WORD MADE FLESH

WORD MADE FLESH

Philosophy, Eros, and Contemporary Tragic Drama

by

GEORGE HUNKA

With an afterword by David Ian Rabey

EyeCorner Press

Word Made Flesh:

Philosophy, Eros, and Contemporary Tragic Drama

Published by EYECORNER PRESS, March 2011

ISBN: 978-87-92633-08-8

Cover design: Denise Avayou

Layout: Camelia Elias

Cover image: "Heart of the Matter," Paul Cava.

Used by permission of the artist.

For Marilyn

and in memory of my father

CONTENTS

Preface for the reader

It is self-evident that nothing concerning art is self-evident anymore, not its inner life, not its relation to the world, not even its right to exist.[1]

Tragedy, both as genre and as consciousness, presupposes a metaphysics. Comedy has not attracted the same philosophical attention (from Aristotle to Eagleton) because comedy is essentially of the empirical world: the material world is the banana peel, man as machine, rising above his station only to be slapped down by the limitations that objecthood, fate and coincidence place in front of him. We don't require a metaphysical rationalization for comedy. It reminds us of our earthbound condition and reconciles us to its whimsical ironies. There is, even in the greatest comedic achievements such as *Twelfth Night* or *The Producers*, a warning to know our place and portion: taking on a pretense of sexual otherness is a hindrance to happy matrimony; the conman is caught upon his own cleverness, in courting failure achieving unwanted success. But those are lessons for this world, not something beyond it.

This is not to say that tragedy requires a system of philosophy any more than comedy does, but in trying to explain the attraction of tragedy—the witnessing of almost unendurable earthly suffering—appeals to reconciliation, levelling lampoon or necessary amusement will not do. The necessity for tragedy will not be found in the same world as comedy, but somewhere beyond, behind. We have few treatises on comedy or the philosophy of com-

---

1 Theodor W. Adorno, *Aesthetic Theory*. Translated by Robert Hullot-Kentor. Minneapolis, MN: University of Minnesota Press, 1977, p. 1.

edy, but of tragedy these are legion. And many, interestingly, are not the product of dramatists but of philosophers. Neither Aristotle, Hegel, Nietzsche, Steiner, Kaufmann nor Eagleton, to name only six who have written at considerable length on the form, is a playwright himself. But all are in one way or another philosophers who found in the tragic consciousness an avenue to metaphysics.

Any radical reconsideration of tragedy may begin even from the expression of a single thought, as complex as that thought might be: *The World as Will and Representation*, its author said, was spun from a single thought; Rudolf Malter has said that it might be posed as: "The world is the self-knowledge of the will."[2] There is in this thought the indissoluble kernel of the tragic consciousness itself. The will can come to our own knowledge as subjects only through that very special object, our own bodies; it is this object that we know most intimately, from inside out, as it were, though we as objects can't readily "know." But we can experience, we can sense, the will operating through the body: it can be recognized though we cannot define it in empirical terms. The evidence of this will, as it were, can be seen in our own experience as well as everywhere else in history and the world: and it is a smoking gun.

The nature of this will, in the tragic consideration, is beyond moral valuations such as optimism and pessimism; these two terms are useless indicators and forecasts of an unknown and unknowable future, which may be welcomed or feared, and they do not speak to the present; in any event, they reek of determinism; and it is the present condition of humanity which is under tragedy's

---

2 Cited in Christopher Janaway, "Introduction," *The Cambridge Companion to Schopenhauer*. New York, NY: Cambridge University Press, 1999, p. 4.

examination. If we live anywhere in time, it is not in the future, but the morphing present, under the shadow of the past. Comedy (like some progressive politics) attempts to slip from this shadow into a sunny meadow, but is this possible, or is this mere illusion as well? The first great tragic work, the *Oresteia*, suggests that with the establishment of earthly justice we live in sunny brilliance and have broken with our bloody pasts. But even the *Oresteia* does not convince, and in any event, the *Libation Bearers* may have been a bone tossed to the elders of Athens in hopes of the annual prize rather than an honest reconciliation.

In *The Death of Tragedy*, George Steiner argues that the genre of classic tragedy in its ancient and Elizabethan forms became untenable in the Enlightenment that followed the 1660 restoration of Charles II, but it took less than three centuries for that Enlightenment to begin devouring itself. Or to finish: the will through its male and female human agents turned against the world in a subatomic form at Hiroshima and Nagasaki, in an administrative form in the camps of Germany and Russia; but certainly, in terms of physical and social science, this was a science determined by Enlightenment values. If one wanted proof of Enlightenment's failure, what more proof could one ask for? Surely this should be enough. (Which renders any talk of "futures" additionally absurd; how many futures were eradicated in Europe and Asia in the years between 1939 and 1945; and as a species we are complicitous in this eradication, for it wasn't Nazis or Manhattan Project scientists in whom the guilt inheres but in the human animal himself, in all of us. How we would like to forget this and blame it on some nation-state, ideologue or quasi-abstract malicious outsider.) This was the judgment, in any case, of Adorno and others of the Critical Theory school. In the wake of the catastrophes of the First World War and those that followed, tragedy was routed, however. The search for justice had for some time been a lodestone of tragic practice; but justice could not be found (nor would it be found, the task was impossible), and so tragedy still awaited new expression for the 20th century. One would have thought that the dark promises of self-knowledge experienced in *Oedipus* and *King Lear* had been fulfilled: that the tragic consciousness would re-emerge with a vengeance.

The single thought, however, continued to live, and it lived most in theatre, because theatre, the unique speaking, bodied self-knowledge of the will, was its most appropriate arena. In the work of Artaud and Grotowski, tunnels were dug under the Disneyland of mass culture in the wake of World War II. In their work the tragic consciousness continued to inhere, and it partook not of rationalist Enlightenment values but of values of the spirit: and they were necessarily tragic, with almost nothing of the comic in the work. (There are no "funny bits" in Antonin Artaud's *To Have Done with the Judgment of God*.) Here, too, the tragic rediscovered its radical roots in the body; it took some time for dramatists to begin seeking a literary, lyrical text appropriate for the stage.

But they have begun, some years later, to do so. Completing the circle, some dramatists have begun to create a philosophical theatre once again, a theatre that is rooted in the metaphysics of tragedy.

Some notes here in the spirit of Adorno: evidence of the necessity for tragedy in the twenty-first century. And perhaps the irrelevance and blindness of unthinking comedy.

Preface for the author

The performance of this drama, whose scope of time by earthly measure would comprise about ten evenings, is intended for a theater on Mars. Theatergoers in this world would not be able to endure it. For it is blood of their blood, and its contents are from those unreal, inconceivable years, those years that no waking consciousness can apprehend, that are inaccessible to any memory and preserved only in a gory dream, those years in which operetta figures enacted the tragedy of mankind.[3]

A dream of a theatre. Collectively, the entries here are not a manifesto nor a theory. It is neither an academic treatise (for it lacks the apparatus that would make it useful as such) nor a textbook. It is presented here largely as it occurred to me over the seven years of its composition, winding here and there: a single thought as it emerged in the thinking. And in the body that produced that thought. I have honed and sharpened, but otherwise have left it unstructured, for it tends to no real end.

What destruction is sought is a destruction of received consciousness, not a bomb thrown into a building or a classroom, and the feelings expressed are far too self-contradictory to constitute a theory that can be of any practical use to anyone, least of all its author. They describe a theatre that does not exist, that may never exist except as an imaginative possibility in the mind of the dreamer.

---

3 Karl Kraus, *The Last Days of Mankind*. Translated by Alexander Gode and Sue Ellen Wright; abridged and edited by Frederick Ungar. New York: Frederick Ungar Publishing Co., 1974, p. 3.

If there is any urban locus here, it is a curious one. The philosophy and work under consideration are not fictive, but they are fragmented, the individuals responsible distant from each other in both space and time. Perhaps their work is best considered as the dim candle lights that shone through the windows of monasteries, perceived from a distance in the night, and as in the Middle Ages examples of a work and toil that goes on in the dark. And they do manage to leave their mark on the night, as the ascetics of the Middle Ages left their mark on history through their manuscripts and translations, coming down to us from another era, even another world. Seen from above, these dim lights are just visible here and there, loose constellations on a dark continent beneath. Perhaps these ascetics work ignorant of each other, but during the day they may conduct travels and pilgrimages, and return with a new knowledge and a faith that, in their work, they are not alone in the world, however dark the night, however great the intervening physical distance. They are community in thought, if impossible in body.

At the same time, they leap across genre. Like the pre-Socratic philosophers, whose work took the form of fragment, aphorism and poem, one can't say that a single text is drama, this poetry, this philosophy. The lyrical beauty that courses through the pre-Socratics is the same as the beauty that courses through Beckett and Celan. So, too, it would be wrong to limit this ascetic hallucination to writers alone. Actresses and actors, designers, directors may constitute additional points in these constellations.

They also constitute the quotidian fragments of which a dream of the theatre can be built. For it is a fever-dream within the skull (like the black-box theatre itself), fed like any dream by shards of the non-dreaming experience. From these dreams are constructed cathedrals, stone by experiential stone. These would eventually hold and store the manuscripts and performances, wrought with obsessional intent and discipline, for which the cities and culture do not necessarily care. The women and men of the monastery, not seeking fame or recognition, necessarily living hand-to-mouth, expecting neither payment, approval nor gratitude, have the sole desire to keep the dreams of the imagination alive, in a culture which would gladly have them criminalized or killed as a means of keeping the ideological and religious peace.

In the night air one might hear from these monasteries the catch in the throat of a woman's orgasmic cry, smell the sweat of the male body, experienced then inscribed within the dramatic text and by the dramatic body—both of which arise from the bodies and imaginations which the words of the manuscript render viable and visible as the performed drama. It is a dream of theatre that we will not see in our lifetime, that our sons and daughters will likely not see in theirs, given the direction in which history seems to be moving: deeper into industry, administration, puritanism and materialism, producing the real, bright exposure of the catastrophes that have introduced a post-human age.

To put the names of individual artists to the candle lights would be presumptive here, not only because they may be inferred by the material presented, but also because the list would be incomplete: they define themselves in their work and intent, and they may desire to remain in the night, the more easily to conduct their work. Dream work is private and secret, even the description of the dream is intimate, shared only among those whom one feels secure and safe in communicating—there are dire risks involved, revelations and intimacies. But the description of the dream in drama remains necessary. Among the most important legacies that parents can leave to their children is the continuation of that dream, that such investigations are of enormous value in the dark world: a dream is a parent's gift of love to a child, who may make further careful, personal steps to its realization.

Word Made Flesh

§ 1

Tragedy lies at the origin of theatre and the origin of philosophy. Contemporaneous with Aeschylus, Sophocles and Euripides were the pre-Socratics, including Heraclitus; the *Poetics* of Aristotle did not appear until at least two generations after the *Oedipus*, Plato's *Republic* about fifty years after the death of Sophocles.

Tragedy lies, too, at the nexus of the Judeo-Christian Word, the Logos, and the representational sexed body. Hesiod, of the sixth century BC, saw the foundation of the world (and consciousness, and Imagination itself) as the product of a metaphysical, mythological sexual congress, quite apart from the authoritarian, all-encompassing consciousness of the Judeo-Christian deity:

> In truth, first of all came Expanse; and then
> wide-bosomed Earth, seat ever safe of all
> the immortals who hold the heights of snowy Olympus,
> and murky Tartarus in the recesses of the wide-pathed land,
> and Love, who is fairest among the immortal gods,
> loosener of limbs, who in the breasts of all gods and all men
> overcomes thought and prudent purposing.
> From Expanse came Darkness and black Night;
> and from Night came Ether and Day
> whom she conceived and bore after joining with Darkness in
> love.[4]

---

4 Cited in Jonathan Barnes, *Early Greek Philosophy*. Second edition. New York: Penguin Books, 2001, p. 3-4.

"Love ... overcomes thought and prudent purposing": the eruption of the Irrational at the moment of consciousness' birth from night and darkness. It was this Irrationality that Plato and Aristotle sought to repress (and therefore the repression, too, of the tragic in Plato's *Republic*, as well as the rationalism of Aristotle's otherwise far-from-simple discussion of the form). The origin of the Judeo-Christian tradition lies with the authoritarian creator of Genesis 1, but also with the creation myth contained in the first chapter of the Gospel of John:

> In the beginning was the Word, and the Word was with God, and the Word was God. The same was in the beginning with God. All things were made by him; and without him was not any thing made that was made. In him was life; and the life was the light of men. And the light shineth in darkness; and the darkness comprehended it not.

The light of consciousness is bodied, then, in Logos: word as life, the light of men.

If theatre is sick, then the sickness is a lack: the lack of the forgotten origin of the art. Between the eruption of the Irrational force surveyed in the pre-Socratics and its suppression in Socrates and Plato lies the period of the great Greek tragedies, the basis of theatre and drama. If we worry that our examination of the tragic origins of the questioning consciousness is somehow ancient, recidivist, we must remember that the 2500 years between the time of the ancient Greeks and our own time is but the fraction of the time it takes to blink an eye, in relation to the long evolution of the race; even shorter than that, in the expanse of time and space of the cosmos. Even if it weren't: necessity consigns all contemplation of past and future to the immediate present. Science and technology may have progressed, but the bodied senses of consciousness have not. Nor, as Freud propounded, have we been able to suppress that Irrational force that leads to both ecstatic pleasure and ecstatic suffering, our awareness of which constitutes that original Beckettian sin of having been born.

Given this, why should tragedy be impossible now, as so many contemporary commentators on the form have it? The title of George Steiner's *The Death of Tragedy* speaks for itself, and even one of tragedy's most revealing recent theorists, Walter Kaufmann, said in 1968:

> [Contemporary playwrights] who try to write tragedies always run the risk of approximating contemporary architects who put up Gothic buildings. Whether they construct good copies or variations, their work cannot claim true excellence. Doing something really new and interesting with a form in which such great masters have performed so many towering experiments is so difficult that success in any number of other genres is much more probable. ... In comedy untried possibilities abound. It would be exceedingly surprising if the next hundred years should produce tragedies as great as the best we have. But they might well produce comedies as brilliant as any.[5]

This, it seems to me, is surrender: a form of sour grapes, an unnecessary, cowardly and ultimately foolish rejection of possibility and imagination. In any event, it will not be for us to judge success and excellence (though critics egocentrically try to speak to some vague and ideologically-constructed standard); as any theatre artist knows, it is the here-and-now, and not posterity, with which we are concerned. Comedies we have, and we will

---

5 Walter Kaufmann, *Tragedy and Philosophy*. Princeton, NJ: Princeton University Press, 1968, p. 358.

continue to have. But if we are to have a theatre whole and well, we need those tragedies too, those tragedies that reach for the torturous wonder at the cosmos and the lives and movements and language of men and women, the wonder that gave birth to tragedy and philosophy. In an age when both are desiccated, perhaps that coupling, too, can again give our theatre health.

§ 2

Schopenhauer's radicalism did not lie in the metaphysics laid out in the first book of *The World as Will and Representation*—it is a distilled and corrected Kantianism that can be found there, and Schopenhauer paid his debt to it.[6] Apart from his personal example explored by Nietzsche in "Schopenhauer as Educator," it lay instead in three things: first, his identification of the will as the thing-in-itself (as dark as this is, it is not for that reason invalid or untrue); second, his placing of aesthetic experience above that of science or abstract philosophy as the means to experience of the noumenal; and third, his integration of Eastern philosophies into his own Western tradition. But it is the ironic fate of visionary radicals like Schopenhauer that history has its joke: for it is necessarily incomplete at the time of its writing. Schopenhauer had completed the first volume of his magnum opus in 1818, a time during which the bloody recognitions of the French Revolution were fresh in the European mind, and the Industrial Revolution was just beginning. As newly industrialized

---

6 Kant's principle achievement was in positing a quintessentially unknowable "thing-in-itself," a *noumena*, that existed behind the world of empirical existence and its *phenomena*. Schopenhauer believed that he was completing Kant's distinction when he posited that the *noumena* could best be described as an unconscious, all-encompassing "will," which he distinguished from that of mankind's phenomenal volition, though this was the expression of the noumenal will in the empirical world.

cities experienced their explosive growth in the following two decades, Modernism itself emerged as a peculiarly democratic and urban response in the work of Baudelaire and Büchner, both of whom were likely directly influenced by Schopenhauer's philosophy. The poet and the playwright set out to accomplish in art what Schopenhauer had accomplished in philosophy: an event which Schopenhauer, with his favoring of art over science, would certainly have approved.

But this urbanization and industrialization also called for new economics and new psychology which emerged with the formal theory of communism and class struggle of Karl Marx and the exhilarating psychological findings of Sigmund Freud. The years 1818-1914 were a time of relative peace in Europe; Marx's surplus value (which Bataille would later reconfigure as excess or plethora) was absorbed by the growth of the cities and capital itself. But, as Bataille suggested, this excess energy created by industrialism and capitalism would burst from their limits: too large for the cities and the banks, it would then emerge as war or in some other manner. Ultimately, in 1945, its energy would literally explode, laying waste to Hiroshima and Nagasaki in Asia; its administrative energy in the system of the concentration and death camps scattered through central Europe.

These were phenomenal manifestations of the Schopenhauerian thing-in-itself as well, and in their wake the place of art and community needed to be wholly reconceived (the sociological, psychological and aesthetic project of the Frankfurt School under Horkheimer and Adorno). But this reconception would take place in a culture in which Schopenhauer's visions had come to obvious fruition. It was Adorno's project to suggest how to philosophize and make art in the shadow of these manifestations;

Bataille's to reconceive art and community. In both, Eros, not Thanatos, provides the guiding spirit of any possible redemption, in the dark shadows of the drive to death that Freud described. This is the historical and philosophical situation in which tragedy's necessity became more and more acute, as both Adorno and Bataille well recognized. It was an urgent call for music and drama, the two greatest art forms, to be reconceived under these new shadows. Married to Schopenhauer's radical thought, it suggests a new tragedy for the twenty-first century.

In comedy the anxiety of the self is dissipated in laughter; in melodrama, in tears; in agitprop, in anger. In tragedy it finds a silence in which the self is forced to turn inward, its anxiety pure and complete; it is faced full, without escape.

§ 3

In *The Metaphysical Vision*, Ulrich Pothast describes Schopenhauer's conception of tragedy and its relationship to Samuel Beckett's plays and novels, but also provides a broader relationship to contemporary drama, underscoring Schopenhauer's radical understanding of the form and providing a basis for its relevance to contemporary tragedy.

Apart from music, which is a special case, tragic poetry represents the highest objectification of the knowledge that is available to us about the Thing-in-itself, the will. "Tragedy," Pothast writes, "gives a view of this life stressing that life is essentially suffering and leads finally to death. It belongs to the arts which try to give a near replica of a [Platonic] Idea; in tragedy, this is the Idea of the human being. ... Only in tragedy is the Idea of human being presented as a living *and dying* person—to the effect that the value and nature of life as well as of death can be seen clearer than anywhere else."[7]

The knowledge and recognition of death and suffering are at the center of all tragedy: but, in opposition to Aristotle, this knowledge is not necessarily accompanied by catharsis; the knowledge itself is the experiential product of tragic experience. "It is not fear and sympathy with the individual heroes of the tragic action which are to be induced," Pothast continues, "but rather, in the tragedy's characters *as well as in the spectators*, a new kind of knowledge: the knowledge that individual existence in the world of appearances is thoroughly deceptive and that, therefore, individual death is unimportant, being nothing more than an illusion fading away. This knowledge allows the characters to free themselves from the drive of their individual will, and it allows the spectators to temporarily acquire the same attitude of freedom, a kind of happiness. ... Therefore, one can say that in Schopenhauer's theory of tragedy, suffering and death of the leading characters become the inspiring genius of a philosophical world view in the spectators. The tragic action enables them to renounce their normal affirmation of the Will-to-life and to temporarily find a new attitude of freedom and calmness."[8] (Emphasis added.)

Knowledge in the Schopenhauerian sense is not empirical knowledge of the world through science or documentary, but an experienced, bodied knowledge of the individual self: a knowledge available only through art, not philosophy, which partici-

---

7 Ulrich Pothast, *The Metaphysical Vision: Arthur Schopenhauer's Philosophy of Art and Life and Samuel Beckett's Own Way to Make Use of It*. New York: Peter Lang, 2008, p. 68.

8 Pothast, *op. cit.*, pp. 70-71.

pates in the arena of rational concepts. This is thoroughly consistent with Schopenhauer's emphasis on experience rather than abstract intellectualism as the source of knowledge. When the extremes of some contemporary tragedy are examined for their value to the individual spectator, such as in Howard Barker, Sarah Kane and David Rudkin, it must be said that this knowledge—necessary, as Pothast suggests, for the true autonomous freedom of the individual, including the freedom to turn the will against itself—is the sublime product of contemporary tragedy. This knowledge is unavailable to contemporary comic irony, which undermines this knowledge by providing, through camp or a facile wink at the audience, plausible deniability of that knowledge: it is all a joke, if we wish it so. It is too easy to turn away from this knowledge (which is, it must also be stressed, not *truth* in the sense that it is a final declaration of philosophical meaning).

The sexually desiring and desirous human body is the highest phenomenal representation of the will as it acts through the world of objects, according to Schopenhauer; there is an implicit link between this and his concept of tragedy as the highest (with the exception of music) of the arts. The contemporary tragedians named above render this connection explicit, linking ecstatic sensuality to a knowledge of death and through this knowledge achieving a form of freedom. This is an amoral project, if it is the knowledge of the will that is gained. Schopenhauer's terminology here is problematic: in our time, the word "will" is associated with volition, but it must be remembered that the word itself is a necessarily imperfect description of that empirically indescribable thing-in-itself. Schopenhauer's concept is of an *unconscious* force or activity: a will, to coin a term, without volition and operating through the human body in both sexuality and suffering; and without this volition, the will becomes something beyond ethics and morality. It suggests a constant conflict between the will and its objectification in the world. It is this conflict itself which constitutes the formal basis of tragedy.

There are formal and technical consequences to this neo-Schopenhauerian critique as well. "We must keep in mind," Pothast writes, "that the logic of dramatic action in Schopenhauer's view of tragedy totally conforms to the logic of empirical events which are experienced by well-identified individuals in the forms of time, space and causality. It is through their *knowledge*, induced by the tragic action, that the tragic characters can free themselves from the bounds of individual existence and see through the veil of Maya. And only this knowledge also enables them to adopt the new attitude of resignation in which they even accept their individual death and give up their lives 'cheerfully and willingly.'"[9] Traditional narrative and theatrical forms participate in "the logic of empirical events" that inhere to the telling of a traditional story, which then becomes just another manifestation of the veil of Maya that must be torn apart to gain recognition of the thing-in-itself behind all things. But the description of empirical events doesn't provide access to the knowledge that the tragic experience suggests. The neo-Schopenhauerian tragedy and its characters destroy these forms in the path to knowledge.

The relationship between repudiation and resignation must also be discussed in terms of the "contemplation" that belongs, according to Schopenhauer, to the true work of art.

---

9 Pothast, *op. cit.*, p. 71.

§ 4

The active contemplation for which the art of tragedy aims rehearses a contest between the noumenal and phenomenal. All of theatre's tools are phenomenal—the body, the word, the scene; time, space and causality—but it is only with these that the noumenal can be suggested, hinted at. The metaphysical union of subject and object in the ecstatic moment of recognition is impossible in the phenomenal world. But this tension presents to the spectator an opportunity for the contemplation of other worldly and phenomenal possibilities. It is a contemplation from within this attempted union, not outside of it, and for all its impossibility it nonetheless limns the thing-in-itself of the body and the word.

All the more reason for the spectator to resist *losing herself* in the story, a blindness: this is the Culture Industry's desire. Instead the spectator is engaged in a project to *find herself*, in an attempt to unite with the performer, in its lyrical duration ...

§ 5

Melancholia (or, to call it by its more 20th century name, depression) is cheerfully described as a mental illness to be cured on the psychoanalytic couches and from within the medicine cabinets revised and retained by the Culture Industry. Surely, it is a condition: common and extensive enough to deserve Robert Burton's 1621 *The Anatomy of Melancholy* (an impressive 1,382 pages in the NYRB Classics series); it is the height of the Culture Industry's mechanistic optimism that these thirteen hundred pages might be rendered irrelevant with the prescription of the proper pill.

Melancholy is not a quality solely of tragedy. Twenty years before Burton, Shakespeare's Jaques in *As You Like It* casts a pall over the marriages in the final scene when he declines an invitation to stay in the forest of Arden and opts instead for the spiritual life. No doubt he is a spoilsport. But it underscores the isolation of the melancholic spirit; it also points the way to the more ambivalent romances and tragedies that were just to follow; and the chill cast over the final scene is real.

Jaques' decision is that of the man or woman who sees as a life's work the mapping of the abyss. Perhaps it is a disease—perhaps a prescription for Celexa would ameliorate Jaques' darkness and permit him the dance of Act V. On the other hand, his isolation would not leave us with a slightly bitter taste if it were not somehow possessed of some kind of truth.

Let us turn the tables for a moment and suggest that melancholia is not a disease but rather a condition of spiritual health, the necessary product of the full acceptance of Schopenhauer's single thought: a metaphysical condition of knowledge, not a mental and physical sickness. All tragic artists work from a condition of this melancholia, and the tragic imagination emerges from it. Julia Kristeva writes in *Black Sun*, her study of depression and melancholia:

> For those who are racked by melancholia, writing about it would have meaning only if writing sprang out of that very melancholia. I am trying to address an abyss of sorrow, a noncommunicable grief that at times, and often on a long-term basis, lays claims upon us to the extent of having us lose all interest in words, actions, and even life itself. ...

> Rather than seek the meaning of despair (it is either obvious or metaphysical), let us acknowledge that there is meaning only in despair. The child king becomes irredeemably sad before uttering his first words; this is because he has been irrevocably, desperately separated from the mother, a loss that causes him to try and find her again, along with other objects of love, first in the imagination, then in words. Semiology, concerned as it is with the zero degree of symbolism, is unavoidably led to ponder over not only the amatory state but its corollary as well, melancholia; at the same time it observes that if there is no writing other than the amorous, there is no imagination that is not, overtly or secretly, melancholy.[10]

What is found after this journey through melancholia, especially with another, is knowledge, and it is a knowledge that is not merely intellectual, but sensual, sexual and metaphysical: the joy of this knowledge is hard-won, as Oedipus, Antony, Cleopatra, Tristan and Isolde will attest, and at times it is won at the loss of phenomenal existence, in the brief moments of noumenal union available to us in the world of representation. (The comedy, wit and humor is similarly hard-won: and therefore more true. It is this kind of comedy that we find in Lear's Fool and the gravediggers of *Hamlet*: a wit that magnifies, not diminishes or ameliorates, the tragic consciousness that animates these plays.)

In the art of contemporary tragedy, this journey through melancholy is mapped through the long periods of Morton Feldman and dark expanses of Mark Rothko, the broad negative spaces of Alberto Giacometti, the plays and novels of Beckett after *How It Is*: and there is a beauty in it not available to comedy as a genre, because the melancholy is utterly without respite. But it is essen-

---

10 Julia Kristeva, *Black Sun: Depression and Melancholia*. New York: Columbia University Press, 1989, pp. 3, 5-6.

tial. Melancholy is denied in the products of the Culture Industry, especially in those of its theatre, where the melancholic project should be bodied and spoken, shared with the fleshed bodies that share the room with us. It is as if, in the wake of the unparalleled catastrophes of the twentieth century, we have turned resolutely away from the truths that melancholy and despair offer us, and also away from the profound and sublime joys and ecstasies that may emanate from the knowledge and experience the melancholic journey suggests.

It is not melancholy or depression that is the sickness; it is the palliatives offered by the Culture Industry that constitute the disease; we welcome it and ask it to wrack our bodies into a laughing stupor and call ourselves amused and happy. And it is this disease that kills the theatre, the dramatists who write it, the performers who enact it and the audiences that attend it. Tragedy is its antidote.

§ 6

The theatre is my representation. There is no more certain knowledge, once achieved, than this: that the theatre, like the world, is a re-presentation of objects and events that I assemble in my consciousness, and mine alone, for each individual's consciousness is his or her autonomous possession. I witness a theatrical event from my own personal physical perspective, seeing the stage and its arrangements of bodies, objects and events from a unique physical and perceptual vantage point. It is true that I am a body among bodies, placed within a collective audience, but this does not mitigate my essential isolation, for my response is preconditioned by this status as individual object, as a unique vision of a perceiving subject. Our language here gives us away, as always. "I feel pity for him"; "I think this play is good (or bad)"; "I desire that actress's body; see how she displays it to me"; "I am bored (or excited, or exhausted)"; "I don't think that actor's performance is very good"—all of these, in their linguistic constructs, reveal the essential uniqueness of our perspective, the subject "I" of the grammatical structure, my own construction of the theatrical elements presented for me, and once the performers, designers and dramatists have let the play loose, it is mine. The theatre is my representation.

Once this realization, with all its horrifying, isolating, exhilarating and ecstatic possibilities, has been experienced, it cannot be unexperienced, unlearned, unrealized, and it will color all my theatre and theatrical experience from then on. Only the hard press of voluntary, willful ignorance—and this is not uncommon, some of us fear our own bodies and desires more than anything else in this world—will be able to eradicate this realization from my consciousness. I remain a member of what is called the collective of the audience, or the collective of the experience, but I now define myself as simultaneously a constituent and opponent of it. I gauge my reaction, consciously and unconsciously, from within that collective, from my privileged unique perspective. I am also aware that my own perspective is colored by the culture of that collective: not merely the aesthetic and cultural perceptions with which I enter the theatre, but as an individual body amongst other individual bodies, sharing perceptual tools such as the eyes and the ears. Though ultimately it is not through their eyes and ears with which I witness the play, but through my own. Like Creon, Antigone and the chorus of Sophocles' tragedy, I am empathetic and antipathetic to the collective simultaneously (any chance of ultimate reconciliation between these is illusory;

violence unutterably and always follows upon violence, whether Creon or Antigone's perspective is privileged, the play would end in slaughter in either case, witnessed by the silent and in any event illusory gods). I am always a unique and individual object, when alone or with others, but the collective is a mere abstraction and does not exist without the voluntary or involuntary gathering of several individual bodies within one space at one time. For this reason my individual perspective becomes primary, the *primus inter pares* in the individual/collective dichotomy.

If I were a performer rather than an audience member, I would still experience the theatre as my representation, and whether I am an individual member of a theatrical company or a member of the audience, this experience is identical. On stage I move my body through space among objects and other bodies, and my movement and perspective remain unique. His *lehrstücke*, Brecht insisted, were learning plays not for the audience (at least not primarily for the audience), but for those who performed in them. As cast member too I remain individual. If the theatre remains my representation, we have an understanding of the perspective of cast members of Richard Foreman's plays, for example, many of whom have told me they feel no more utterly and fully themselves as individuals than when they appear in one of his productions. Finally there is the evidence of performers of other contemporary work, which demonstrates the untapped resources that can be called into practice once (but not before) the realization of the theatre as my representation occurs.

My theatre is then charged with desire, disgust, fear, ecstasy, possibility from each moment to each moment. The origin and nature of this charge will become clear later in this work, but it is a charge which both unites and separates auditor and audience, spectator and performer, performer and performer, in a process of seduction. Theatre is there and not there, always passing, explicit and present only in my representation and my body's status as privileged object. What differentiates the theatre from the world is its disciplined self-consciousness as the object of my representation. It knows itself to be an art, a lie that tells my singular truth. Stephen Greenblatt aimed at this in his book *Shakespearen Negotiations:*

> [The theatre is] a fraudulent institution that never pretends to be anything but fraudulent, an institution which calls forth what is not, that signifies absence, that transforms the literal into the metaphorical, that evacuates everything it represents.[11]

Once the representation is evacuated, my imagination rushes into it. Possibilities form, and all that is necessary is the courage to explore them.

§ 7

The condition of the exile. My apartment on the Lower East Side of Manhattan is about a quarter-mile directly south of the block of Clinton Street where my grandfather Maksym Hunka first resided when he arrived in the United States in 1914 at the age of 22. He arrived in Manhattan from Berezhany, a city in the Ternopil oblast in Ukraine, which was at the time a territory of the Austro-Hungarian Empire within the Austrian region. A linguistic exile in his own country, speaking Ukrainian, he fled to America (family legend has it) in an attempt to escape the draft for World War I. Eventually, he went to Philadelphia where he be-

---

11 Stephen Greenblatt, *Shakespearean Negotiations*. Berkeley, CA: University of California Press, 1989, p. 127.

came an electrician and raised a family. He never returned, to my knowledge, to either New York or to Ukraine for the rest of his life, though he remained in touch with a brother and sister in Ternopil through the end of his days. I don't believe he was ever comfortable speaking English and I don't remember him ever speaking it well.

The status of the immigrant or exile is often neither voluntary nor involuntary but some combination of both; but it can be a status which one seizes as a possession of the self or attempts to shed in the desire to determine that one is finally at home. The empirical circumstances of my own birth render me by international law an American, and living in New York I am home, by some culturally-determined diktat. But I am also very much a European, even an Austrian, by any number of standards, and I seize upon this identity as a means of defining the aesthetic, intellectual and spiritual conditions in which I choose to identify my own provisional home (for however illusory, we must have such an idea): exile, in this example, by choice, but not entirely so. For there is a matter of taste and style in saying that, on merely an aesthetic level, I find European work more congenial to my interests. This is not a value or a moral judgment, only the observation of a trait that I've noted in myself through the years. For it's a ludicrous and ridiculous proposition to value or validate the work that emerges from one continent as in any way superior or inferior to that of another. It is to our liking and it speaks to us more than others; that is all.

The self-defined, self-aware exile has a special access to the sense of the uncanny that produces art—a reference to the German equivalent that Freud uses, *das Unheimliche*, the "un-homely." The artist is never truly at home in his work, but is engaged perhaps in an unsuccessful search for home (at least, in America, which promises a new home for the immigrant). It may be the special curse of American drama today that this search for home possesses all of the cowardly anxiety and fear that accompanies an act of desperation. Ultimately this home is imposed rather than found, an artificial construct that provides an illusory blanket of security. *Our Town* is an examination of a home, for better or worse, but Grovers Corners is indeed not our home but only a condition of illusion, what comfort or security other than that the community has constructed from a bare stage, a ladder and several dozen chairs? The lie is exploded when it is realized that this is merely a representation of a home, but truly it is anything but a home. The artist in self-aware exile knows that home will not be found and explores instead the anxiety and catastrophe that undermine the idea, the sentiment of the home-sweet-home. There is no "good night" at the end of the day, only additional dream or nightmare.

The phrase "to be at home in one's body" acquires a problematic status for the exiled artist engaged in the performance of dance, music or theatre, for this awareness of exile carries through to the experience of one's own phenomenal body in exile from the noumena. The performer through discipline seeks to use the body as a bridge across the chasm of phenomena and noumena, the empirical and the unquantifiable, ultimately to express the possibility for the at-oneness, or atonement, that would erase this separation.

The performer seizes the status of exile for his or her own self-becoming, exploring its unending dialectics, not in a wandering for a static home but for a dynamic in which imagination and possibility have their free play: anything but home, unless home is the realm of the impermanent. (So the permanent marking and transfigurations of the body, too, are a hopeless search for that static home.) The suffering and ecstasy in that realm of the transitory possess the nights in the performing body, in the theatre ...

§ 8

"The only philosophy which can be responsibly practised in the face of despair is the attempt to contemplate all things as they would present themselves from the standpoint of redemption."[12] In Adorno's construction one finds all kinds of loaded words but the remainder of this last entry in *Minima Moralia* may surprise in that it centers on that seemingly innocuous word "standpoint." But standpoint, perspective, position, is the basic condition of theatre: the audience ever outside performers, the dyadic relationship of spectator and actor. A culture which objectifies all of us as things to be marketed, even as we consider marketing ourselves, renders us as purchasers and purchased, the central and essential post-capitalist dyad. As Adorno mentions it is a hopeless task: he continues by saying that we cannot escape this dyad today: "... it is ... the utterly impossible thing, because it presupposes a standpoint removed, even though by a hair's breadth, from the scope of existence, whereas we well know that any possible knowledge must not only be first wrested from what is, if it shall hold good, but is also marked, for this very reason, by the same distortion and indigence which it seeks to escape."[13] Redemption is not only meaningless ("the question of the reality or unreality of redemption itself hardly matters"), but impossible.

---

12 Theodor Adorno, *Minima Moralia: Reflections on a Damaged Life*. Translated by E.F.N. Jephcott. New York: Verso, 2005, p.247.

13 *Ibid.*

The same holds true for live performance, but there are other avenues, other processes than to rip apart the fabric, the tight perpendicularity of the performative weave; there is a movement inward rather than a movement out, towards union rather than separation. Movement itself, dynamics of politics or metaphysics or spirit, is always open to inspection and investigation, as Brecht's project indicates. The trip can be mapped, and the map can indicate untaken paths towards the interior of the continent of the self. The cartographer must be precise and observant lest he provide maps that are useless to fellow travellers, but one gets better with time. Some become very good indeed, and those that do allow their impulses and instincts, trained by discipline, to imagine the lay of the land; they open the land to their audience as a singularity that contradicts, even as it expresses, the dyad of theatrical experience.

Exiles bring themselves, voluntarily or via compulsion, to live in strange lands, external or internal, for which they may have very incomplete maps indeed (perhaps they only hint at the shape, suppleness and contours of the landscape), lands which they internalize as they explore. The dream of redemption (or atonement) is to find in this land of exile a home away from home, impossible and meaningless perhaps, but a condition to be attempted nonetheless, so that the face of despair is not the only one we ever find ourselves able to recognize; to glimpse and recognize, perhaps, the face of joy.

§ 9

Ways of knowing/seeing/hearing. In exploring the beginnings of perception and of art we also explore its outermost limits. Schopenhauer's elucidation and extension of Kant's delineation of the limits of the phenomenal world reach back to First Perceptions, First Questions: what we experience through the sensory apparatus which is our body, how we experience it. To the corrected Kant, experience of the phenomenon is constrained by the *a priori* precepts of time, space, and causality: succession, position, and motivation, B's reactions to A's own existence in this given framework of perception, back beyond which and towards its furthest extent one touches on the noumenal, on the thing-in-itself (the Will, in Schopenhauer's construct), or what lies behind the Hindu *maya*. An empiricism that denies this noumenal (as so much empiricism does; it was the frightening implications of the continuing philosophical probing beyond these seeming phenomenal limits that gave rise to the foolishness of utilitarianism) abandons the philosophical obligation to continue asking "Why?", to abandon the wonder that any existence at all is possible, this wonder the first principle of philosophy itself.

These first precepts are, as well, the basis of all that is known and knowable, and not merely the preconditions of art but certainly the preconditions of an empirical science of consciousness. It has become clear over the last century that the Hegelian project has failed in the effort to restore science and art to the unity which it found in the early pre-Socratic philosophers, and which gave rise to the notion of tragedy itself. The emergence of Cartesian dualism in the first half of the seventeenth century dealt a death blow to Western tragedy, which found its wildest and most extreme expression in Shakespeare and the Jacobeans. (Shakespeare dies in 1616; Descartes' *Meditations on First Philosophy* is published in 1641; the English theatre closes under Puritan rule in 1642. A chain of causation? Probably not. But a notable coincidence, if not. There is a sense in which Cartesian empiricism would make it utterly impossible for the ruined, weak, hungry, shattered, dying Lear to have the strength, at the end of act five, to "reenter ... with Cordelia dead in his arms"; phenomenally impossible, but noumenally necessary. Beckett considered *King Lear* utterly unstagable, and it could be that in a world before Descartes this wasn't the case; in a world after Descartes and empiricism, this is the case.)

Kant and Schopenhauer revolutionized perception, a revolution with has yet to have its full effect. But even the empirical sciences in recent years have begun to correct their original dismissal of transcendental idealism, the original dismissal based in misunderstanding and ridicule; Hegel and Marx were found much more useful to power and authority, and much more prone to easy absorption into academic philosophy; in Kant and Schopenhauer there is too much of the artist. In the July 2002 issue of *Physics Today*, a journal published by the American Institute of Physics, Neil Ribe and Friedrich Steinle cite chaos theorist Mitchell Feigenbaum's conclusion that, after two centuries of dismissal, Goethe in his *Theory of Colors* may have been right all along (Ribe and Steinle also discuss the use of "exploratory experimentation" in contrast to Newtonian investigation, in so doing suggesting avenues for art as well as science). And in his study of Schopenhauer's work, Bryan Magee observes that quantum physics has been finding in Schopenhauer's concept of matter-in-itself as an indescribable nexus of energy a concept that predates contemporary scientific observation by two hundred years. He also notes that, "Ever since the publication in 1941 of Konrad Lorenz's paper 'Kant's Doctrine of the *A Priori* in the Light of Contemporary Biology' more and more biologists of reputation have stressed the Kantian nature of the view of perception towards which modern science is leading us. This is corroborated also by the work of some of the most distinguished of modern psychologists of perception, such as Richard Gregory and Stuart Sutherland. Through the work of such figures as Noam Chomsky it is even finding its way back into philosophy."[14]

The body as what we can call the Prime Object—though as much object as an apple in front of me, nonetheless the only object through which I might intuit that energy known as noumenon—is the basis of first principle in art, and in some new music and theatre we have this rediscovery; their repeated attempts at limning the principles of expression and perception have their roots in this transcendental epistemology and begin to reap the aesthetic benefits of the Schopenhauerian ontology. And this is all based not in some Cloud-cuckoo-land of abstraction, but in the very essence of bodied experience itself. Richard Foreman notes in a 1990 interview the very real basis of this ontology: "I saw a particular static moment from my seat in the Circle in the Square where I watched a rather dreadful production of *The Balcony*. And I remember seeing Shelley Winters, on one side of the stage, and Lee Grant on the other, and it was just a moment of stasis, and a moment of a kind of tension between them, and I just wanted to make a whole play that had nothing except that unresolved tension between them. And I wrote out of that. I said that's what I want in the theater, just that moment, and it doesn't develop into any of the other awful stuff, the psychological stuff, the narrative stuff, the adventure stuff that it always develops into."[15] The "unresolved tension" that Foreman

---

14 Bryan Magee, *The Philosophy of Schopenhauer*, revised and enlarged edition. New York: Oxford University Press, 1997, p. 104.

15 "Ken Jordan Interviews Richard Foreman," 1990, unpaginated. Accessed

investigated has its roots in the time, space, and causality of the Kantian world, and from 1968 through the cessation of his theatrical activity in 2009 he explored its origin, over and over again, not unlike Goethe's method of "exploratory experimentation."

In returning to what he called his project "to return to the true essence of the piano, to its acoustic realities, and to ignore the trivialities of fashion as well as the weight of history," composer Tristan Murail is engaging in the same kinds of exploratory experimentation. Murail uniquely perceives the avant-garde as both a historical and an an-historical locus of investigation. In an essay from 2000, "After-thoughts," Murail identifies one of his principal aims as "research," in the nature of this Goethean project. Sounding not a little like Schopenhauer in his distrust of academicism, Murail writes, "Composers should not be satisfied with music that is simply there to please. They should not allow the style of their music to be dictated by fashions, the easy acceptance of institutions, of orchestras, or of the regular concert going audience. These are not sufficient reasons for writing music, for stealing from the life of another. Unfortunately a number of trends are more and more prevalent in composition today which either ignore the problem of communication, or which—resting on the ambiguous notion of postmodernism and on pseudo-musicologic or pseudo-philosophic discourses—are in fact not much more than disguised academicism." He goes on:

> We are often told that the avant-garde is behind us, that we have achieved so much distance and perspective that only a "post-modern" attitude remains possible. However, in my daily work as a composer this idea is disproved. I continue to search for new

online at http://www.ontological.com/FOREMAN/rfinterviews/Foreman Jordan1990.doc, 7 January 2010.

ideas and materials. Some of this research is on a technical level—clearly the case when speaking of developing new computer programs or new ways to facilitate the comprehension of sonic analyses—but another type of research that I perform daily is purely musical and aesthetic, looking for ways of effectively using the material which I discover to create new sonic/musical objects. By "new," I mean something that I want to say but have not already said, and which no one else has said either. You cannot express original ideas by recycling old material: new thoughts need to be formulated with new material. Our vision of the world has become so historical now that when we speak of the avant-garde, we automatically think of the avant-garde of the nineteen fifties. But if we stick to the etymology of the word, by definition there always will be an "avant-garde" or our civilization is dead. Let's stop being ashamed of this notion!

This position may seem ironic, since at a certain point the "spectral movement" was seen as a reaction against the "avant-garde." And clearly it was a reaction against certain composers who believed that they were the avant-garde. But, in reality, it was a reaction against their refusal to make even the slightest concessions to the phenomena of auditory perception. Abstract combinations on paper are not musical research. As a result, we fought against this type of musical behavior. However, we were not the only ones to criticize that music which was so prevalent during the late-sixties and early seventies. Advocates of the music I referred to above as disguised academicism accused the so-called "avant-garde" of emptying the concert halls and alienating the listeners through their decadence and excesses and, in a certain manner, their criticism was justified. However, one need not respond to these criticisms as they have.[16]

---

16 Tristan Murail, "Afterthoughts," in *Contemporary Music Review*, 19:3, 2000.

Murail, in noting that he explores "the phenomena of auditory perception," is as much a transcendental epistemologist (so far as this is relevant or valid) as Foreman is when he sees bodies reacting to each other, as they make contact via sense. But these explorations find limits, always; and both Murail and Foreman press against these limits as they, unlike the empiricists, keep asking the questions required of philosophy and art: the eternal "Why?"

Theatre can next explore the terror and tragedy of and beyond the phenomenal, and the possibility of bodied renunciation and ecstasy in art and theatre (and lessons for us: in our own bodied experience, to reach and touch the ecstatic sublime). To return, as Foreman and Murail, to first causes, to posit responses to the intuitions of the body in this instrumental condition of tragic perception. Inhering entirely in the instrumental, performative body.

§ 10

"People think that because I do this I am well read and knowledgeable and I know what it means. I have almost no education at all and no idea what it means. I'm not interested in what the plays are about, to be absolutely honest. When I work with Sam we don't analyze the plays at all. My first task is to find the music of it."[17] Billie Whitelaw, in speaking of performing Beckett's late plays, is being disingenuous. There's no doubt that Whitelaw has an innate, textured understanding of Beckett's project, though she claims that she has little interest in books, her conversation is always literate and informed.

---

17 Cited in Jonathan Kalb, *Beckett in Performance*. Cambridge: Cambridge University Press, 1991, p. 17.

But her point here suggests the difficulty of a performer's embracing the ambiguity of theatrical experience in plays which sacrifice understanding and meaning to express a multitude of understandings and meanings; the performance takes place in the empty spaces between alternate interpretations (and even, I will make the argument, when there is no correct interpretation, or a play resists any interpretation). What is the American-trained actor, seemingly condemned to a watered-down Stanislavskian training in the service of naturalism, realism or absurdism (which is, most of the time, mere parody of naturalism and realism), to do? There is a sense in which the late plays of Beckett are the most realistic of realistic plays in denying meaning-making closure. But the American actor, who is trained to find motivation and invent pasts for their fictitious characters, is ill-served by Beckett's late characters: their pasts may be fictions, their motives non-existent, except that they must be on the stage, rehearsing their existences or non-existences, night after night.

But this makes their performances bodied and instinctual, souled, separate from the intellect, and why Beckett's plays can have a greater impact on those who don't attempt to find meaning in them, seeing instead the picture and hearing instead the music; and it is the actor who embodies the image and speaks the music of the play. Beckett's actors should, instead of being confused, be gratified at the opportunity to display themselves instead of hiding behind motive and intellectual understanding. (And the best always do, honestly, which is not to deny them their considerable powers of understanding, only to indicate that these powers may be the least important element of their selves they that bring to a part.) Actors enter fully into a collaboration when they draw the emotions and sensations that their costumes and the lines they're given evoke from their own deepest wellsprings of emotion, not those of the "individual," the integrated but kaleidoscopic monad, that one begins to see in Shakespeare, especially in the middle-period tragedies: one is sorry that Olivier didn't do more Beckett.

A performer must somehow acknowledge multiple consciousnesses at once: the integrity of the performance lies in how they embody the spaces and silences that surround these ambiguities and possibilities. They must feel the spaces and the silences in their bodies. They must define the space around them, use their words to make tender incursions into the silence, as in a painting by Bonnard. The performer is not embodying an integrated character in a logical story, any more than the writer is writing one. Character and story are two of the theatrical conventions with which in the interest of essentials they must dispense. (In any case these are fictions.) They are together, in theatrical space and time and language, exploring aspects and dynamics of the bodied self.

§ 11

The poor Artaudian actor, signalling and screaming through the flames, is no match for the amplified culture of noise. Torture rendered into pathos. A violence-obsessed culture will only absorb the Artaudian performer into its own mill with a satisfied smile: "You are a part of us now, as you always were, knowing it or not." Now that Auschwitz and Hiroshima have been installed into the gallery of televised and iPodded images, the naked screamer scarcely makes a dent. Now the flames are our entertainment; in fact, we digitally superimpose more flames upon these flames in the name of spectacle. We can point out, over and over again, that the screamer is live before us, that the scream is unamplified, but what in the end does that avail us, especially when we've come to expect it?

Although spoken language is a set of symbols and metaphors different from music, spoken language and music share similarities: if composers investigate the harmonics and dynamics of a single note's attack, writers for the stage have access to the phoneme with its own harmonics and dynamics, even if metaphor is grafted atop it. Over duration the musician expresses and investigates the decay of sound and the harmonics available to decay over time. Decay is implied in attack. Music yearns to an impossible primal silence. (Which isn't to say that music and theatre and art can deny this silence with the unending impulsive will to impose noise on the silence, presence on absence. This is what manufactured culture, in the service of the fascistic will to material and economic optimism, does.) Theatre, however, can also investigate, and demonstrate, the urge to decay of our own linguistic symbols and metaphors: the decay of reason and understanding.

The theatre's one true thing regardless of the nature of the performance, comedy or tragedy or else: That spectator and performer alike share in a period of time passing, of physical decay (like that of the decay of a tone, or the fading echo of a phoneme or metaphor), of a movement to corporeal death, together. Theatre that fails to acknowledge this from the moment the curtain rises fails to acknowledge a primal truth about performance; this is not at all escape; the rest of our lives constitute escape from and willful ignorance of this truth. Spoken, bodied language's ability to explore this decay through stillness and silence is only beginning to be recaptured.

The spectral: both a fertile investigation of the spectrum of sound (what it hides among its physiological effects) and a yearning to the condition of the ghost, the spirit.

§ 12

Arc of extremism. The hatred of war and violence is a self-loathing in which we wallow. In protesting against violence and war of any kind I am a hypocrite when I turn to the culture industry and am amused by blood and violence, ceaseless spectacle, on screen, which is how I perceive reality as a twenty-first-century subject. The love of being battered by external image and noise, our peculiar twenty-first-century masochism, the more extreme the industrially-conceived fantasy the more pleasurable our submersion in it. (The argument that we see it as an ironic and satiric comment on the world we create rather than our pleasure in that world itself grows more specious the more we demonstrate our desire to spend our time submerged in that world of violence. We must, on the contrary, create and treasure silence and peace, reject surface for depth. Instead we treasure the flat screen and flat experience.)

All against the conception of human as individual rather than an atom of a mass (the mass the monad for industrial and mass thinking). And more: atomic fragments of a mass now, in the present, having lost not history (for we can't lose that, it's not ours to lose or reject) but historical consciousness, so that all seems new to us and we remain infantile, discovering truths as if for the first time when they've been common in the race for four millennia and more. We flatter ourselves.

§ 13

Rebeginnings: Siva. Beginnings are kaleidoscopic: instead of endless hopeless attempts to find a correct entry one must just make the leap and begin, trusting to chance to contextualize. At least three Creations in Genesis, I'm reminded; and the Four Gospels of the New Testament, all contradictory in their beginnings. And three *Hamlets* at least, at least two *King Lears*.

Our eventual beginning, whatever we might choose, will contextualize itself, the key is to escape interpretation and understanding, the urges to rationalize the myth's mystery, instead accepting possibilities, avoiding the urge to whittle them down to a single origin of sensation that we think will be the correct one. It will be a beginning, if it is ours, make no mistake. But if we keep to the outline we make it won't be ours. It will, really, be the outline's, and no-one's. The writerly act originates in the body, and the body must move, drawn to the source of its invitation to move. If not, if we deny the urge to begin, we engage in a rationalistic Puritanism that denies the myth's power to draw us. What Levi-Strauss says in *The Raw and the Cooked* about the reader of myth is as true of the writer of drama, who "will find himself carried toward that music which is to be found in myth and which, in the complete versions, is preserved not only with its harmony and rhythm but also with that hidden significance that I have sought so laboriously to bring to light, at the risk of depriving it of the power and majesty that cause such a violent emotional response when it is experienced in its original state, hidden away in the depths of a forest of images and signs and still fresh from a bewitching enchantment, since in that form at least nobody can claim to understand it."[18]

Like the mythologist, the dramatist enters the dark, through what break in the woods is immaterial, so long as the exploration begins: all roads lead to the not-home, the not-real, the sensation of the myth. In the case of the bewitching forest, the paths marked only slightly at the start: so many have turned back, so the ground trodden only to various degrees. And all paths into a labyrinth of myth and forest illusory. A boy lost in the woods is only lost if he thinks so. Otherwise, he looks and discovers. The path out to be discovered at leisure.

§ 14

Bare life: Homo sacer. Theatre is the art form that validates the self-aware biological being in the midst of others, in community, even alone on stage surrounded by audience: the perceiving life perceived, judged, examined. It exemplifies Giorgio Agamben's concept of bare life, the state of exception, and the idea that 9/11 posits the permanent condition of the "state of exception" from imperial law, allowing bases like Guantanamo to exist without meaningful protest. That an explicitly masculinist power feels free to establish such possessions of beings without rights or wills, is a unique political, biological, sexual state of exception, the concentration camp domesticated and internalized. (Such possessions are at the mercy of a power which possesses the will, and the ability, to use violence against the vulnerable individual self if offended or desirous of doing so, deliberately, arbitrarily.) The struggle is against this exception, through the ability of the

---

18 Claude Levi-Strauss, *The Raw and the Cooked*. Translated by John and Doreen Weightman. Chicago: University of Chicago Press, 1983, pp. 31-32.

individual biological self to say "no" to being possessed, for bare life to be allowed to operate outward with others, instead of isolated. The refusal to allow Guantanamo inmates counsel or appeal is isolative. Writ large, power behaving as it does after the rise of the corporate totalitarian state, Guantanamo is an extreme symbol of the political self under this state. (A note for the margins: it also symbolizes the state-sanctioned closure of the possibilities posed by the multiform myth: the end of play.)

As theatre holds that biological presence is the basis of its experience, so Agamben's idea of the Biopolitical Self seems a theme worthy of exploration. (Agamben ascribes the origin of this idea to Foucault's *The History of Sexuality*.) Modern totalitarian politics apes theatre, centering the body. Agamben: "The present inquiry concerns precisely this hidden point of intersection between the juridico-institutional and the biopolitical models of power. What this work has had to record among its likely conclusions is precisely that the two analyses cannot be separated, and that the inclusion of bare life in the political realm constitutes the original—if concealed—nucleus of sovereign power. *It can even be said that the production of a biopolitical body is the original activity of sovereign power.* ... Placing biological life at the center of its calculations, the modern State therefore does nothing other than bring to light the secret tie uniting power and bare life, thereby reaffirming the bond (derived from a tenacious correspondence between the modern and the archaic which one encounters in the most diverse spheres) between modern power and the most immemorial of the *arcana imperii*."[19] (Emphasis Agamben.)

---

19 Giorgio Agamben, *Homo Sacer: Sovereign Power and Bare Life*. Translated by Daniel Heller-Roazen. Stanford, CA: Stanford University Press, 1998, p. 5.

The significance of the biopolitical body in the theatrical sphere as an object or subject for contemplation and violent activity is clear. It connects Harold Pinter's work to Edward Bond's and Sarah Kane's, and provides a political aspect to explorations of tragedy and sexuality. To what extent do we allow the language of the state to create our bodies? To create each other? To create our selves? What language do we absorb, do we allow to play or define? If the unconscious is structured like a language, as Lacan posits, how have we allowed the state, or its representatives like corporations (mass media, the telephone and technologies companies that control our access to this seemingly free "Internet"—the cruel, vicious joke that there is such a thing as "virtual" or "online" life, putting life in the hands of a cabal of technologists—the language we absorb from a popular culture that is the creation of the powerful), or its microcosms like the family, to manipulate our language and then our bodies as they exist in our eyes? Each body on stage is an instance of the individual in the state of exception. The theatre examines the decisions that are made in the freedom that remains, to a closer connection to the totalitarian state, or to an escape into human possibility. A field that underlies all art that centers the body, or bare life—an exploration of Agamben's idea through Adorno's aesthetics after the disastrous failure of the project of the Enlightenment: the Enlightenment mind turned against its own failure.

§ 15

Seduction, precision and desire. In his *The Theatre of Howard Barker*, Charles Lamb draws a parallel between the practices of

Stanislavsky and Brecht, underlining the shared perspective of the rationality that informs both:

> Brecht's rationalism, however, performs the same controlling function as Bond's or Edgar's Marxism—it is, theoretically, the organizing principle of his artistic method. When Brecht succeeds in adhering to his ideological purpose, his "representational" experiments are rigged so that open critical response from his audience is circumscribed. All Brecht's fuss with anti-realist, anti-illusionist devices suggests nothing so much as the posturings of a conjuror, persistently demonstrating empty hands, showing the inside of the top hat, revealing both sides of the handkerchief. The implication is that we see everything, no concealment, no tricks—we are in touch with "reality" throughout—all of which facilitates the foisting of an illusion.[20]

Coupled with Stanislavsky's statement to his colleagues in the Moscow Art Theatre upon its foundation—"We are trying to create the first rational, moral, public theatre and it is to this lofty aim we dedicate our lives"—the nineteenth-century rationalist basis for both Brecht's and Stanislavsky's theatre becomes clear. So much for innovation: it's a theatre that belongs in the world of Newtonian physics, not quantum mechanics. What neither artist acknowledges is that theatre is an art of seduction, although that seductive impulse operates in all theater. This acknowledgement of the irrationality of seduction would undermine their own rationalist projects.

Another approach is to welcome and embrace the seductive operation of live performance: to make it explicit, rather than hide it under the rationalist consciousness. Seduction denies ra-

---

20 Charles Lamb, *The Theatre of Howard Barker*. New York: Routledge, 2005, p. 32.

tionalism in the effort to transcend the suffering that the history of rationalism has foisted upon the race: audience and performer join beyond the field of questions, beyond the field of meaning. The rational individual cannot tolerate seduction: it is a giving-up of control, of the illusory integrated self, which is then set free into a field of experiential possibility. Instead of judging behavior and performance, as Brecht insists is necessary, auditor and artist join in accepting and experiencing behavior, widening consciousness instead of limiting it to the same bloodless perspective that led to twentieth-century tragedies of rationalist behavior.

Unfortunately for the twentieth-century anthropocentric rationalist, it also means an irrational acknowledgement of death and violence, of the erotic possibilities of theatrical and aesthetic presentation. (This it shares with the late Elizabethan, the Jacobean theatre.) We should despise a theater we can understand. Theater and drama are not crossword puzzles to be filled in by the audience from clues left by the playwright, the director, the performers. Until we tear down the walls that both Stanislavskian and Brechtian practices validate, the walls that separate us from each other will continue to exist. Given its risk, then, we take not sledgehammers to that wall, but the most precise instruments of invasion: words that seduce. Beckett and Pinter knew this; Barker and Foreman know it. In our careen towards disaster, only the most extraordinary measures will eradicate our perverse yearning for self-torture.

§ 16

"Don't want to, but must": Murderers among us. Fritz Lang's 1931 *M* is a bitter comedy of the period, even physically: the

physiognomies of the characters leap from Grosz's sketchbooks, erasing the differences between virtue and vice, good and evil. Today, particularly, the hysterical search for the killer, a killer who lives in all of us (we search outside ourselves to eradicate evil when we need only turn within), resounds: the hypocrisy of the collective criminal bourgeois organized against an individual criminal bourgeois. A corpulent, smug, legitimate establishment working with a thin, smug, illegitimate establishment: former enemies allies, and uneasy. And our tools turned against us. Airplanes, the science of flight and architecture, religion turned against us, and a lashing out: knives, the trusting innocence of a child, our own bodies and wills turned against us, and a lashing out. Our rational efforts to locate and eradicate the irrational source comic: a bumbling search for the terrorist, a bumbling search for the child sex-murderer, accompanied by bombast and a media-induced panic that roots fear and violent retribution in the soul.

And the punch-line: there is always another, living next door to us, or in ourselves, waiting for its opportunity to leap into the world. This we can't stomach: the searing truth we don't care to face. And so it happens, time and time again, to the end of the world.

According to the tantras, we are in the period of the *kali-yuga*, an age in which sacred teachings have been lost, in which the world and its inhabitants are sunk in a swamp of greed and violence. It was said to have begun when Krishna left the earth in 3102 BCE. Bad news for ameliorists and optimists: the period will last for 360,000 years.

§ 17

The writer's body as instrument of investigation. The dramatist is invisible after the theatrical text is created and passed along to the performer for expression, which begs the question: If the dramatist is not expressing during the performative instant, if her work is perceived to have been finished months or years before, what is she doing there? As profoundly physical as the act of physical performance is, the psychic investigation of the writer demands that she use her body as an open conduit for the perception, investigation, and description of the unconscious Schopenhauerian will that runs through it. The performer expresses; the dramatist reads impressions of representations on her body and describes (and inscribes into a hopelessly inadequate language) the linguistic scrapes and leavings of that will. The dramatist answers the question that is directed to her ("Why your text at all?") with this response: "I leave my markings with what the long culture and history of writing has given to me, adding my own scratchmarks to go a little further along the road to destruction and light: the will offers both." To be fully open and aware of the will's operation the writer's body needs to be as trained and supple, as well-equipped for physical observation as the performer's is well-equipped for physical expression, this training a cleansing of the skin's lenses. The avenues towards transcendence are often those which are most obscured by sloppiness, waste, laziness, carelessness, trivia, and garbage. The noisier the representation, the more precise eye is required; the more inadequate the language to the experience, the more carefully considered word. Every word, from noun and verb to preposition and article, carries with it its own theoretical antonym. The dramatist works against this inherent irony and self-contradiction of language. She keeps trying to express lucidly, without irony. To do so she needs the lucid, limpid eye to still her inscribing, shaking, imperfect hand. Which nonetheless, as physiological expression of the will, is always working against itself. The dramatist writes herself out of her expression and disappears into the performer's body and voice. Nonetheless, she is a bodied presence herself in those words, though invisible, requiring a continuing effort at physical perfection of the perceiving instrument, the writer's body (always aging, always decaying, always at the mercy of the amoral microbe that offers dis-ease).

§ 18

Think/am thought. The Cartesian principle collapses upon itself in an age of identity acquired from mass-distributed digital culture. Performers drop the pretense of speaking a self-generated text, disturbing the illusion of autonomy, by donning earphones before they speak; the question, then, is whether they're repeating to us only what they're hearing, what is being filtered through them by a recording, or by a text generated just prior by another performer, or through the repetition of a popular song's lyrics. The performance's video component serves, similarly, as a basis for physical imitation, becoming a form of live video ("video" containing its implicit subject/object dichotomy; I see, therefore I am; I am seen, therefore I am), blurring the exhibitionist/voyeur *pas de deux* into a single body.

They are spoken, rather than speak; I am written, rather than write. As the simulacra of mass-produced, mass-distributed digital images become ever more our stage of life, all numbers, we give up the analog. Which is not to posit that the analog existence ever was, or can be, particularly positive or superior in and of itself. We are also spoken by our families, our ideologies, our relationships, our culture. It becomes such an ingrained habit that we are unaware of the extent to which this cultural syntax, these vocabularies and appearances, deprive us of the possibilities of self-definition and the freedoms bodied perception can provide.

The truly revolutionary act is to reappropriate language and body, to wrench it (through destructive parody or through a disciplined effort of stripping existence—performance or theatre, this dichotomy too is illusory—of its superfluities) from the institutions, customs, habits, corporations, simulacra—the impositions of definition by institutionalized thinking—which have appropriated them from us (with our permission; it's much easier to give them up for a return of amusement or illusory comfort).

§ 19

Like a breath. About ten years ago, Grove Press published a series of beautifully produced facsimiles of Samuel Beckett's theatrical notebooks: the prompt copies he prepared as he readied himself to direct his own plays. Over the last thirty years or so of his life, Beckett had opportunity to direct most of his own work; before making the mistake of calling these the "definitive" productions of these plays, we should remember that Beckett himself never characterized them so. They were, instead, the versions of the plays as the author himself envisioned them at the time they were produced, always with the reminder that even an author's attitude to his or her own work changes over time, and that Beckett revised his own plays and productions as he revisited the texts. Cavils that Beckett considered these productions final, set in stone, dictatorially correct, are conclusions borne of poorly-informed rumor about the man's own processes (rumor adequately scotched with only a little research into the matter) and the behavior of the Beckett estate (hardly attributable to the man himself, dead these past two decades).

The notebooks are an interesting resource for determining a directorial process to a lyrical stage minimalism. Beckett's preparation included his own memorization and annotation of the text before he entered the rehearsal hall: study and consideration not only of the language, but of light, color, the texture of costumes. (Beckett had a keen eye and ear, trained over many years of studying art history and music; his attitude towards color, shadow, texture, and body placement was as considered as Caravaggio's or Friedrich's. And he worked closely with designers and technicians of similar temperament and background, constantly seeking their suggestions and input as to the achievement of a particular effect.) The notebooks are filled with sketches and arrows indicating movement, often as precise as an architect's blueprint.

Even for the short plays, the rehearsal process was a period of long experiment, but not an experimentation of blocking or design; Beckett was quite clear about the expectations he had for the concrete, inorganic aspects of theatrical production. So these details of design and blocking were already determined by the time rehearsals began. Instead, Beckett worked with actors as he would work with musicians (Beckett was an accomplished amateur pianist). His performers were to be off-book when rehearsals began, so that no time would be wasted in rote memorization. This Beckett considered work that could, and should, be completed before the first day of rehearsal. Instead, the weeks of rehearsal were dedicated to physicalizing the language, Beckett working intimately with the performers, shaping the physicality of the work in very close collaboration with well-trained performers.

Beckett took the trouble to hand-write the full text in these notebooks, notating with precision, to the syllable, where pauses and silences and changes of tone should occur. If Beckett was a director who made unusual demands of precision and physical movement from his actors (not unlike Grotowski and Foreman), he demanded the same precision and care from his own thinking about a staged text; his crabbed handwriting, in these autograph pages, reveals an unbending service to the text, even as he treated it as the mere origin for a fully staged realization, to be completed by the performer, who would, after all, end up vocalizing these pauses, silences, and tones, every pause as performed as a word.

If one has studied music one is familiar with notation and annotation, and the peculiarities of twentieth-century music are, in some cases, far more open to performative creativity and expression than those of earlier music. It's interesting, too, that in discussing Beckett's work, actors and actresses tend to access musical, not psychological, terms. Veteran Beckett performer David Warrilow has gone so far as to say, "I barely deal with psychological reality. ... What works is finding what musicians have called the 'right tone.' By 'right' I mean what works for me. I then have to trust that it'll work for somebody else—that if I get it right, if I sing it 'on key,' 'in tune,' it's going to vibrate properly for somebody else. ... When the note is not quite 'on,' it makes me physically uncomfortable, it makes me nervous, it doesn't sit right, I start to get negative feedback from my system."[21]

---

21 Kalb, *op. cit.*, p. 60.

To gauge the kind of creativity that Beckett sought in his actors and actresses, one can turn to the musical scores of Beckett's contemporaries and near-contemporaries. I'm thinking particularly here of Schoenberg and Webern, whose extraordinarily precise scores nonetheless reveal entrances for a performer's creativity.

In the music of both composers, one finds small notations. Above a chord or a short passage, Webern might write, "in parenthesis," or "left hand like a mysterious drum," or "more!" How does one play such things? The final chord of Schoenberg's *Sechs Kleine Klavierstücke* should be played, the composer tells us, "like a breath." How does a pianist strike this chord with this explicit exhalation? But this is where the performer brings his or her training, talent, sympathy for the score, to the performance, and no two performances are identical: the breath is individual. So, too, for a lyrical theatre that grants the performer new autonomy.

§ 20

Elsewhere. I'm less and less interested in plays and writings about theatre, more and more in other disciplines. In thinking of the writer's body as an instrumental eye, realistic and naturalistic dramatic texts don't serve. The language lacks muscle and sinew, flesh and sensation. There is a disconnect between language and writer's body; the pen could have written these without a hand's guidance.

Language and body merged. The words, and the gesture, opening a catastrophic eye. In her preface to Bataille's *Inner Experience*, translator Leslie Anne Boldt clarifies Bataille's sometimes too gnomic expression: "In fusion [of one and other], the subject is absent, the object is dissolved in continuity, yet this continuity is radically outside of any continuity which a discontinuous being might envisage. It is NIGHT, but a night which 'is' not—a night which can only be apprehended by a vision which has been decentered, rendered 'ex-orbitant' by the emptying of its contents into the abyss of non-knowledge. The eye is a privileged image in Bataille's texts. In the appropriation of an image during the course of normal vision *[or 'normal,' traditional drama—GH]*, the blind spot where the rays of light intersect is of little consequence. It is both a place of non-being (on its own, it can generate no image) and the site where the power of vision is concentrated (where the elements of image are condensed). It is of great consequence, however, at the moment of fusion: when the stores of knowledge are released, the blind spot of the eye is dilated. In it, knowledge is absorbed into the NIGHT of non-knowledge—the intersection of rays opens violently in a movement of catastrophe."[22]

Theatrically and performatively, the eye of the body is reflective of the spectator; looking deeply into it, as in a yogic contemplation and meditation, one sees the darkness of the dilated blind spot: the notion of attraction and the gravity of night, a black hole of attempted perception that absorbs and swallows all around it. All language a seduction into it. So the performative body tricks and seduces, an extraordinarily transgressive, revolutionary invitation, an invitation into the "abyss of the unknown," an unknown with a very individual quality because shaped, in vision, by the *principium individuationis* (the same principle which is undermined and destroyed by Dionysian union) of the individu-

---

22 Georges Bataille, *Inner Experience*. Translated and with an introduction by Leslie Anne Boldt. Albany, NY: SUNY Press, 1988, p. xviii-xix.

al's body (hence its transgression: to let go, to release, the known, in expectation of an experience that suggests the ability to glimpse the erotic wounds of tragedy; it is only suggestion because ultimately metaphoric, though the urge to escape from this metaphor is the truly theatrical experience). One talks of the pleasure of theatre. But pleasure and pain are a dichotomy arising from the subject/object relationship. In the quotidian world they are antipodal. In ecstatic fusion they are one. Though theatre, and perhaps all art, can do nothing more than suggest, to exemplify, the fusion, because publicly performative, nonetheless this is why theatre is not mere fun, entertainment: it is religious, psychic, spiritual. And why precise discipline and cleansing of the writer's passive eye, the performer's active eye (all body, all skin, eye), is the foundation of its exercise.

This clearly has practical effects and consequences in terms of health, in terms of linguistic and gestural discipline. Beckett's directorial process a distillation of Grotowski's in many ways, a distillation that focuses, laserlike and with enormous precision and subtlety, on the body's performance of linguistic expression. So it is a basis not only for a dramatic theme and philosophy, but also a preface to a book of its directorial, compositional, dramaturgic, and design practice.

§ 21

Once removed. The re-presented human body, in such intense manipulated fakery as theatre and photography, suggests a crucible for the experience of desire and torture, a straining of the possible against the impossible, once removed: representation and metaphor themselves the space of art, manipulation and language themselves the vehicles of removal. Perhaps these were the elephants in the room that Artaud and Grotowski tried so vociferously and intensely to deny, in so far as their work was fated to fail. As invested and inspired with religion and mysticism as their work was, it lacked the one aspect of religion and mysticism that all sects share: the spoken prayer. (Even if Artaud prayed in his essays and poetry, he loathed prayer on the stage, preferring the scream instead.) At the very least this prayer was subordinated to an illusory performative freedom. To make language count we make a leap of faith, participate in a suspension of disbelief and pretend that there is a "magic" to it: an intonation and precise vocabulary that, spoken in the correct order and at the right speed, will lead us to a state of suspension when we can feel the body's release into a realm where detachment and immanence is possible. And this is common illusion that we buy tickets for; it is only possible in the twin vehicles of sacrifice and orgasm that Bataille describes; but art can merely suggest. True transfiguration is beyond visibility, so beyond the theatre, or photography, or art. Stage darkness is an absence of light; even in black the boards creak as the performers sneak on and off stage. Real darkness is a pure absence, an absence even of black.

In a very crude fashion art is an assembly manual which tells you how to put the experience together, but no assembly manual is substitution for the thing assembled. Perhaps you are all thumbs or in cutting corners you decide to not tighten the screws (saves time, and stands well enough without it), to replace a missing part with some sloppily applied glue (it will look the same, but the structure is compromised; it won't last). But even the simplest assembled experience requires patience and precision. Unfortunately the most profound aesthetic experience is built from an assembly manual that describes the creation of an impossible structure. In the Charles Ives piano score for his 1921 song "Duty," there appears a chord made up of 11 notes. Perhaps prayer, or self, is what suggests that this 11th note can be struck as precisely and with as much attention, with as much intention, as the other ten.

The dramatist's body, my body, is also crucible, as much as performer's, but has the additional burden of requiring the qualities of a spectrometer, which must be as blind, without prejudice or fear, and exactly sensitive to the experience it measures, that sensitivity requiring as precise adjustment to express linguistically, to shape new prayer, as the performer's to express, to audibly articulate and embody new prayer.

§ 22

Desire transformative: Golding's Ovid. Shakespeare was fully aware of the ability of desire to transform not only object but subject: Golding's 1567 translation of the *Metamorphoses* was a neverending source of inspiration for his work. (And not only Shakespeare; Ezra Pound called Golding's Ovid "the most beautiful book in the language.") This and other Renaissance translations gave birth to the extraordinarily sensuous flowering of the English tongue in the sixteenth and seventeenth centuries, culminating in the achievement of the Jacobean drama and, in verse, John Donne. In looking back at this poetry we see what we have lost in materialist speculation. Was it, ultimately, Bacon and Newton (and Hobbes and Smith, who sought to put society, economics and politics as the same rationalist footing as Newtonian physics) whom we have to blame the coarse denial of the senses' possibilities? The limitation to scientific and logical rather than souled and supple instrumentation. (And the difference between

Bach's exercises and the music of earlier Renaissance composers such as Machaut and Biber, Bach's passions and masses another story.) The Internet, the cell phone, the iPod only the most recent instances of the replacement of the disintegrating, the tender, the ever-dying human body with the technic of rationalism and wires.

The flesh always prone to transformation, ecstatic decay and metamorphosis. (Yes, even now: improvements in medicine have not changed the integrity of bodily possibility, only its manipulation; Shakespeare's body, Ovid's, Daphne's, Adam and Eve's the same as ours; Shakespeare and Ovid's transformations imaginable in Daphne's, as even Justine's body is self-imagined in, and as, de Sade's own, as Jean Paulhan helpfully points out in his preface to *Justine*.) But this slippery reptilian sensuality is the birth of the English language's suggestive possibilities, and the redemption from suffering and stasis that desire offers.

§ 23

The artist as advocate: paradox. How evident, obvious, and self-centered is the public isolate, the artist, in the theatre or any other art. Those who rage against their publics; what is it about Austrians like Bernhard and Kraus that they turn against their own country so? Perhaps a too-close recognition that the great human disasters of the century were their own. They counsel isolation and silence but enter theatres and concert halls, write and orate. And every art work, every performance, even those that take the form of something other than essay or aphorism, is a work of theory, a theory of perception. Each is philosophy, like it or not; and most conform to the philosophy of the day, conformity rewarded with success, one must only turn up the corner of a work of art to see the philosophical and social conventions that lie beneath its surface. The most revolutionary art today, the art that strives for silence and solitude, compassion and love, is worn down and chewed up by the press and the closed-minded audience, rendered ridiculous: the work of art considered as the cheap Molotov cocktail thrown by a wild-haired, black-coated anarchist through the window of a bank. Though this does not happen much any more, not with safety glass, modern science has rendered transparency no longer brittle but as strong as a plate of steel. And about as effective as that, as a revolutionary gesture.

§ 24

Get out your handkerchiefs. Art has neither use nor morality. To posit that it is utile is to place the aesthetic experience on the perceptual level of yet another wrench in the toolbox that constitutes the utilitarian approach; to posit that it is moral is to abstract puritanical castles-in-the-air from the contemplation of the individual aesthetic object; worse, that these objects (including the body, or its activities) can be perceptible as good or evil. The moralist (be he Rousseau or John Gardner) who makes these distinctions never fails to place himself on the side of the angels; like God, who could also rationalize his creation of "evil" as a means of recognizing "good," he is sure he knows evil where he sees it.

We may wish to get out our handkerchiefs as we contemplate the damage that the knowledgeless will leaves in its wake, but emotion and self-expression (whatever is expressed, it is not "self") are not elements of the aesthetic event, which is experience and recognition. Emotion arises secondarily from the expression, from our capacity for compassion. The artist who laughs at his own jokes, or weeps at his own elegies, is a panderer, imposing on the audience the proper response to his work. It is the Broadway musical, the Hollywood film. One need only recognize the great performer as one who serves as a vehicle not for the writer's words, or the director's "concept," but as a corporeal expression of the intimations of the will that her body allows her, these intimations provoked by, but not identical to, the expression of the writer, the composer (in the phenomenal world objects and selves, as we commonly understand them, are by definition separate; it is not the composer or the writer who is expressed through the performer's body, but her own recognition of the energy released by their suggestions; in this her integrity and strength and creativity inheres). Selflessness lies, by definition, beyond the reach of emotion. And only selflessness expresses the phenomenal dynamic of the noumenal.

The concept of the "noble savage" suggests a basic "goodness" in humankind that suffocates all expression of any kind. (One can only think that Rousseau spent far too little time among savages, but in the savage world, the simplest morality inheres: that which is good keeps me alive, that which is bad destroys me. How wonderfully utile, that. And how ignorant of the nature of the "me.") One seeks the amelioration of social ills in institutions; that is what we have governments for, not art. If we turn art into one more ameliorist institution, we have destroyed it, and its possibilities.

Turning the question around: What is society's obligation to the artist (which is as the question should be, for political and cultural power inheres in community, not the individual)? Society's obligation is to provide freedom for these transgressive explorations. Art has no role, or use, or value, to society, for society prefers to destroy the transgressive artist as a means of guaranteeing its safety, conceit, and power. (The individual is another matter; elective affinity operates not between mass and individual, but between individual and individual.) The artist remains separate and alone, to see the world whole, and to offer this world to a society that, as a mob most enamored of its innate "goodness" and self-worth, couldn't care less.

§ 25

Make no mistake. In rejecting dead surfaces and the media—literature, theatre, music that keeps us on artificial life support, insisting that in pretending to mean they communicate, and their elicitation of easy laughter that wraps us in the illusion that we have authority over our own lives—we reach once again for the true power that surges through our bodies, the power to self-define and limn our desires and significance for ourselves. We make no mistake in turning vision and hearing inward. Eros demands that we take The One by the hand with us. Performance is a metaphor for it.

Tragedy undermines satire, as the erotic undermines the ironic. In the ecstatic moment the epiphanies of music and language shift the ground beneath our feet. The lyrical insidiously and quietly worms through and weakens tyranny. The work of revolution and freedom is done in small rooms, in whispers, movement approaching stillness, sound approaching silence: the groundwork of freedom must be laid out of the sight and hearing of those of the virtuous tyrant, who arms himself with money and power. In protecting himself he thinks he is protecting everyone.

§ 26

Neutral. A community which despises the tragic experience, the tragic artist, has a number of means of castration at its disposal. The first (and most recent, and effective) is absorption: an ideological absorption that posits art as ameliorative therapy, the place of art as therapist's couch (once the community has laid the artist down on it, with seeming love and respect, out come the knives). The second is denial of privacy and solitude to the artist (as privacy and solitude are no longer considered as places of contemplation but of alienation; privacy and solitude now for sale to the highest post-capitalist bidder, marketing and advertising driven by fear), so that the work cannot be done at all; to bury the artist in the same trivia of the day as forms the insulation of the community from an awareness of death. The third is pointless ridicule; faced with tragedy, the community cannot be silent, but is impelled to drown tragic expression in minor sniping, in marginalization, in mischaracterizing tragedy as a pessimism rather than a valid experiential perspective. The fourth is to accuse the artist of isolating himself when, in truth, it is the community which isolates the tragic artist (through attack, or ridicule, or deafening disinterest). As tragedy is an experience of the individual self, the mob despises it. The fifth is to define tragedy as irrelevant to contemporary experience (and in a culture which defines worth as something of practical application, as what can be read from a price tag, in art's digestibility as comfort food, this accusation of irrelevance may be the most damning).

In defense, the artist needs to spit on the hand that holds the knife. In isolation, in the midst of a ridicule which expresses itself in silence, disinterest, and snarky dismissal, the tragic artist recriminalizes herself: the tragic art, transgressive against optimism, progressivism, trivia, and easy amusement, is a crime that saves. She cannot expect company or success, and her rededication, in the midst of loneliness, fear, and intense burning pain of consciousness and frozen social identity, must arise from a belief, a faith, in tragedy's necessity, and the possibility of a healing love, which is mined from its near impossibility and improbability, and is tragedy's message. The pain that sears is a symptom that the spirit and the body have an unmet need, the artist's obligation to find a way of meeting that need. (An entire lifetime can be experienced without meeting this need; the loneliness is real and terrifying; when possibility arises it must be hungrily embraced.) Tragedy is a life, not an art, craft, genre, trope, or career. It requires discipline, daily rededication, concentration, 24 hours a day and seven days a week, in the face of culture's indifference. It is something the artist lives within: her art and life consubstantial. Hence her violent defense. In that profound loneliness, she fights, or dies.

§ 27

Brecht's failure. Revolutions are hatched in small dim rooms, haunted by yellow light and crouched bodies, among the few, in whispers. Not in stadiums, in boxing rings, on television, or on the stage of Lincoln Center. The revolution of perspective and consciousness that precedes any social revolution: the world can't be transformed until it is seen anew: recognition of possibilities that emerge from within. Otherwise regurgitation of stupidity and suffering. And even then, there are no guarantees: most revolutions fail, especially those content to repeat the culture's acquired and all too easily replicable tropes of revolution, let alone the rest.

§ 28

The dream of the theatre. After Brecht, I can't talk about the magic of theatre, whether the magician is David Copperfield or Penn and Teller: evocative of empty virtuosity, the empty "Ah!" that turns us into children instead of reawakening what of a child's play and enjoyment in play remains in us as sensuous adults. (So long as all our moments remain within us, we can draw it forth, if we allow it.) And it is that first thoughtless astonishment that most people are talking about when they think of "the magic of theatre" (smoke and mirrors, partners of bread and circuses): subsumation of self smothered under spectacle. Empty spectacle robs us of our will to change; we place ourselves in the hands of the magician and become the perfect subjects for the totalitarian, fascistic state, of conservative or radical/liberal persuasion. Magic is a one-way street.

But the dream is two-way, paradoxically it reaches a hand outward to touch the world in its conscious expression. Most theatre is a card trick. It should be talking in our half-sleep, our unconscious so close to the surface that it emerges from us in a language that bridges sleep and waking, unconscious and conscious, dream/nightmare and the asphalt street, beyond conscious interpretation so that it can only be heard.

Lying on the surface of our unconscious: blood, lighthouses, a reach for the Other. In *The Interpretation of Dreams* Freud writes of our sleeping bodies' physiological reaction to the words and images that we dream. If grasping, we reach; if frightened, our heartbeat quickens and we shiver. Perhaps we try to run, in the fine irony of our condition our body wants to escape what transpires within our skull. If desirous, our body also responds, and warms.

I distrust magic in the theatre. I don't want to be tricked. In being fooled, I am insulted. I want to be invited, not struck over the head by some mallet wielded by an overpaid illusionist with a warehouse of hidden cards and cheap tricks up his sleeve. Theatre allows us to enter the structure of our dreams, points out perspective, what lies behind the word, how it changes. Spectator and artist become one in the recognition and exploration of the unconscious. It is, at its root, aesthetic, a word with its origin in the Greek words *aisthetikos* (sense perception), *aistheta* (perceptible things), *aisthanesthai* (to perceive). Far from abstract, aesthetic feels the world through its flesh. It wakens; leave the anesthetic for the circus.

§ 29

Let x equal x. In *Negative Dialectics* Adorno retracted what he'd said earlier about the possibility of writing poetry after Auschwitz. "Perennial suffering has as much right to expression as a tortured man has to scream," he wrote. "Hence it may have been wrong to say that after Auschwitz you could no longer write poems."[23] ("Poems" a stand-in for artistic expression generally, Adorno engaging in synecdoche here: plays no longer staged, music no longer composed, dance no longer choreographed, paintings no longer executed.) We might be tempted to excuse Adorno's earlier hyperbolic, mandarin edict from the mountain as a reaction to the circumstances of sudden exile, not only from Europe but also from the Enlightenment that Europe represented.

---

23 Theodor W. Adorno, *Negative Dialectics*. Translated by E.B. Ashton. New York: Seabury Press, 1973, p. 362.

But he was right in both respects; the poetry and culture that came after the events of the 1940s could not but recognize those events as symptoms of a new, dark culture, the portal into the dark through which the race as a whole had willingly stepped. (And Wagner and Brecht and Schoenberg and Webern and Schiele and so many others foresaw this step, and we are still unwilling, many of us, to grant them that: the artists of Weimar become urgent messengers of what is being lost.) To say that these events were mere repetition of events of the past is a willing suspension of historical consciousness itself (never mind a suspension of disbelief, this is a suspension of belief): to posit that the cannon, the gallows, the single-shot rifle, the guillotine and the musket were only the death camps, the Ukrainian famine and the atomic bomb writ small is a value- and history-free conclusion that has excused all the continuing suffering that has followed in its wake: the development of napalm, Cambodia, Darfur, and I speak here only of the suffering that humans have visited on other humans, let alone the life of nature generally.

That the bureaucratic, post-capitalist corporation, in the form of business and government entities, had taken the place of the church and the feudal system in organizing this suffering along lines laid out in organization charts, rationalized by advances in the social sciences, was a qualitative, not quantitative, change in the culture that the race had built up around it. It seems to be generally recognized that the consciousness that created the suffering of the 1940s must be radically realigned if that suffering is to be prevented once again. But even as we repeat the cliche that it must not happen again, the culture industry burrows the race deeper into darkness. It also makes the division of ideologies, the labeling of ourselves as progressive, or liberal, or conservative, or reactionary within that consciousness, a rearrangement of deck chairs on the Hindenberg, already alight and burning. If it hasn't crashed yet, its destruction is inevitable.

Or we engage in the algebra of suffering and amelioration, looking at science and culture as a continuing quantitative balance: let *x* equal the suffering that science has brought to the race, *y* the amelioration of suffering via medicine and agriculture. Is the product of 2*x* (*x* representing here the summary execution of a homosexual, or Gypsy, or Shiite Muslim, or an afternoon at Abu Ghraib) equal to that of 1.5*y* (*y* representing here a mother's love, or the courage of a man who leaps upon another who has fallen into the path of a subway train, or the boon of digital communication)? This is a Swiftian endeavor straight out of the third book of *Gulliver's Travels*. It fails in that it ignores historical consciousness entirely, a historical consciousness that is a proper element not only of culture, but most certainly of theatre, music, dance, poetry, and painting.

This isn't to say that all post-Holocaust art must somehow reference the Holocaust. But it must look back to that suffering and our role in it, and not merely in our ancestors' and our roles as victims, but as torturers as well. To paraphrase Adorno: You desire evidence as to the darkness of the world that culture has created; now you have the twentieth century. What more evidence do you need?

"The concept of a resurrection of culture after Auschwitz is illusory and senseless," Adorno continues, "and for that reason every work of art that does come into being is forced to pay a bitter price. But because the world has outlived its own demise *it needs art as its unconscious chronicle*."[24] (Emphasis added.) The poet, composer, performer elicits this unconscious in the service of recognition: the expression of suffering is a form of remembrance of its victims past and acknowledgement of its victims present. Or the poet, composer, performer buries that unconscious more deeply, in trivia and spectacle and the detritus of a culture industry that is peppered through it, the artist excusing its presence as a form of contemporeity or youth, in denying historical consciousness again: not only rewriting history, but erasing it, as Soviet newspaper editors, with their airbrushes, erased inconvenient personages from archival photographs.

A new revived consciousness, an exploration of unconsciousness, may provide hope, even if it's illusory, even if it's impossible. But all conventional morality and ethics and culture, which we have pretended to rebuild since 1945, as if this same morality and ethics and culture didn't lead directly to the events of 1945 themselves, will need to be undermined and overturned, from the most basic unit of human contact and communication (that between two human beings) to the most complex (that between individual and community). Art is its expression, irreducable to algebraic equation. (A corollary: Use of language, sound, body in art must also be ruthlessly re-examined, changed, shorn of ease and convention. A post-Holocaust art will not sound or look the same as pre-Holocaust art, in any case; it can't, if it's to provide that unconscious chronicle of what has changed, is changing: through our bodies, what passes through them, and the sounds

24 Theodor W. Adorno, *Can One Live After Auschwitz? A Philosophical Reader*. Edited by Rolf Tiedemann. Stanford, CA: Stanford University Press, 2003, p. xvi.

we make, the words we use, the images we paint. Intelligibility of artistic expression is the construct of culture as well.)

Those who call themselves artists need to take all this into consideration at every moment of creation. An apology (or apologia), then, for dour seriousness, or for an anti-illusory aesthetic. But I think I am right. The stakes are higher now.

§ 30

Responsibility. Each word I write and gesture I draw in the air is autobiography, and presents one story to the world. Our time is the only time we have to us, the only time knowable, the only time forgettable, the only time that we have to waste. The history that converges upon the point that is my self is something I can't be held responsible for: but I carry it, it is my burden, and I'm obliged to know it. Each of us has only the time that emanates outward from our gestures, words and art (history inheres and informs, but it doesn't end there). And it sears, as no history can. Why we must grasp our time, it is neither inferior nor superior, but it is different, from all others, in that it is ours. The live performance, dying in silence, is its most profound demonstration.

§ 31

You say you want a revolution. A lesson of the twentieth century: the revolution is best aestheticized, its origin in the subjective trace of the body, not the body's objectification as a sheerly political or social being. Revolution's failures inhere in their ignorance of this, that politics and society (and their most basic construct, the family, the most intimate communitarian structure of both society and tragedy) are not exclusive but afflict the body with stakes that paralyze. In fact one might say that the urgent need is to embody the revolutionary consciousness in our flesh and individual perspective.

The fear that the culture industry instills in the interest of its own economic well-being, its own hegemony, puritanizes us. One can trace this recognition in the theatre by studying the provenance of dramatic revolution from Ibsen to Brecht; Brecht demystifies in the interest of political revolution, then is shattered by the events of the Second World War (after which his two major works in the few years remaining to him in his own theatre, in his East Berlin Soviet, are the remarkable *Buckow Elegies* and his adaptation of Lenz's *The Tutor*, far more ambivalent about the efficacy of purely political radicalism than the *Lehrstücke*). Beckett completes the demystification of theatre and dramatic practice by dismantling even the Hegelian Absolute in which Brecht found succor, his aesthetic a brushfire that clears the field. Foreman and Barker rebuild on this nothing that Beckett left as a new beginning, a new start. (And this is merely the twentieth century, I leave out here the aesthetic revolutions of the Jacobeans prior to the English Civil War, Beaumarchais prior to the French Revolution, Büchner prior to the revolutions of 1848.)

This proves nothing, its validity, as all critical and theoretical constructs, in question as every criticism and theory contains within it the seeds of its own contradiction. Proof is in the bodied performative experience. The spectator takes this example (not a demonstration; this is not an instruction manual) or leaves it be, as he wishes. But the true criminal, the true revolutionary, operates outwards, from the wound, ex-presses it. As revolution is more deeply aestheticized, so is politics. This is cyclical. The frightening but liberating loss of security that is demonstrated in

Brecht's, Beckett's, Foreman's work suggests that our bodies inhabit a contemporary version of the 1920s and 1950s, that the disasters of 1930s Europe, 1960s Asia are pointing to another perhaps final disaster just around the corner. If art is the canary in the coalmine, then our effort to demonize the unfamiliar is a form of strangling the bird with our bare hands when the bird would have died soon enough anyway. We must find a new way of leaping into our pleasure from the expression of our pain, abandoning a desiccated morality, based in post-capitalist possession and the emotional retrogressions and puritanical social structures that provide its support, that which keeps us from an experience and recognition of the noumena, our at-onement with the unconscious as a conscious being.

§ 32

"Thus, suffering crosses the organs of sense, creates hybrids, produces the labial eye."[25] In Osip Mandelstam's "Conversation about Dante," the structure of the *Comedy* is compared to the structure and integrity of a body, the human body that produced it, but also a fully integrated object of its own: "I come to the conclusion that the entire poem is one single unified and indivisible stanza," he writes. "Or, to be more exact, not a stanza but a crystallographic shape, that is, a body."[26] Mandelstam also points up the importance of textiles, particularly in the form of carpets and weavings, in Dante's work. It is suggestive of the use of costume; far more important than a pretty set is the effect of textile on the performer's body, the feel and grace of the clothes she wears,

---

25 Osip Mandelstam, *The Selected Poems of Osip Mandelstam*. Translated by Clarence Brown and W.S. Merwin. New York: NYRB Classics, 2004, p. 116.

26 *Ibid.*, p. 116.

which draw from the flesh itself a shape and drapery that magnify and express, the performer master of movement and the arc of the cloth that moves, breathes over the space of the stage. More power to the performer, less to the set designer (though this also gives the light designer something more to do). On the Broadway stage the sets are often applauded when the curtain goes up. Those sets, unlike costumes, are devoid of a human body within, of course: a part of prettiness. Though sets can be beautiful and important, they are, more often than not, in all too many respects in too many shows, irrelevancies, and if irrelevant they should be dispensed with in a bow to the centrality of the performative body.

Fashion, costume, is a different matter entirely. Language clothes poetic expression, language emerges from sensation in hopes that alchemically this sensation can be demonstrated to the hearer in the form of language (for language is not sensation itself, only expressive and suggestive of it, and language inevitably fails, it can only describe sensation, it must always fail to be identical with sensation, because it is not sensation). But the writer's sensation through language is affected by the language she uses, as the performer's sensation through movement and sound is affected by the feel and touch of the clothes she wears. *Le mot juste* is as essential to a performative transaction between performer and auditor as the pleat of a skirt or the drape of a shirt is essential to a performative transaction between performer and spectator. It is how the poet moves in language that creates a viable, living text; it is how the performer moves in costume that creates a viable, living gesture.

If the performer expresses beauty, she must feel beautiful; if pain, she must feel pained; if vulnerable, her costume must express and stand in for vulnerability. Part of the theatricalness of theatre, this artful presentation of the body, clothing is body's metaphor as language is the spirit's. We don't wander the streets naked, in terms of public presentation our wardrobes tell us what we are, how we think of ourselves, what we wish to tell each other of ourselves, and because theatre is another form of public presentation costume does the same, our bodies move through and with the textiles with which they're adorned. As a poem moves through and with the words and structures in which it is draped.

§ 33

Tailoring a theatre, or an approach to the theatre, to the young, or to the old, or to any given group of people, is an exclusionary tactic aimed at denying the essential humanity of the individuals who compose that audience: an act of xenophobic hatred that demonizes those it excludes, an act of homogenization that tragedy abhors. Tragedy's locus is the individual, alone and in searing pain. Tragedy chastises and liberates the individual, not a demographic group.

Tragedy reaches towards the abstract in the theatrical attempt to use the phenomenal world to limn the outlines of the noumenal. It is more instructive to urge theatre to the condition of music—not as music's inferior or superior cousin, but as its linguistic performative parallel (as music uses performed sound, dance uses performed movement). The precision and discipline we demand of music and dance, of poetry and painting; this precision and discipline, essential to music and dance's expressiveness, are regarded as hindrances in theatre. This demonstrates theatre's self-loathing: taking pride in its sloppiness, theatre has given up tragedy to music and poetry and lazes about in empty amusement, which doesn't require either precision or discipline. It only requires a decision to be blind to theatre's possibilities. It only requires a mass urge to a dull psychosis with all the appeal of attention deficit disorder writ on the artistic impulse. No wonder people don't want it. They don't need it; it feeds no hunger, no matter how successfully it is marketed.

As sounds are symbols (signifying a network of associations that arise within us as we hear them), so are words (a network of assumptions and associations no less and no more complex as those of sounds); music, a collection of these sounds through time, and theatre, a collection of these words through time. A phrase of music is as evocative of memory and sensibility as a sentence, a group of spoken words; Proust demonstrated this a century ago with Vinteuil's composition and theatre still abhors the demonstration (none of that lovely fun that theatre must have, or be considered dead; never mind that in a dead theatre corpses can be led to dance and laugh, too; in fact, it's expected of them). As recorded music is no substitute for live musical performance, television or film are not adequate substitutes for theatre. There are far more similarities between music and theatre than differences. But if that is denied, so is that need for discipline and precision. We're wrong if we think that Vinteuil's music, performed sloppily or without discipline or virtuosity, has the same effect.

A playwright invents a new structure or subverts a genre, a story, or narrative, or sequence of events through which she presents her words as she hears them in her head; a composer invents a structure, or subverts an existing structure, in which to order as far as she sees fit the sounds she hears. The sonata form, the symphony, the theme and variations; the comedy, the farce, the tragedy, also form existing structures to be twisted, into which the performer is invited to play. The performer invites the spectator, intimately, into that play. Intimacy, a seduction between two people, is a far more dangerous field than a performer bewitching a crowd in the service of her ideology: an ideology of the sclerotic elderly, or aesthetic conservativeness; an ideology of easy progressiveness, of the self-love and self-congratulation of youth. This field is the field of a theatre which can subvert and undermine authority: the authority of the politician, the director, even the author; which can transform consciousness. The other may amuse. But it will never have the ability to change the world, an individual consciousness at a time.

§ 34

Étant Donnés. Duchamp's work is an end for the twentieth century, a beginning for the twenty-first: a means of recapturing the aesthetic experience for the individual, alone; a revolutionary experience in a museum, an experience which returns the recognition of our own consciousness to us. (Like a play, the work can be experienced only *in situ*; it may be the most profoundly elitist work of art; reproduction of the experience in other media is impossible.) In rendering the spectator a lone voyeur, the installation fractures the conceit of the spectator as an objective, meaning-making consciousness: the work renders the viewer complicit, as complicit in transgression as the exhibitionistic subject. The spread-eagled woman throws us back on ourselves, our eyes travelling also to the light which illuminates her, the landscape behind her, but always drawn back to the naked, perhaps waiting, figure.

Étant Donnés provokes nothing but questions; in its nihilistic refusal to provide closure on the experience, it haunts: we take away from the work our status as voyeurs and must cope with guilt, or shame, or revulsion, or pleasure, or ecstasy on our own. We cannot share the moment with any companion, the construction of the piece does not allow it. The peepholes draw our human curiosity; the image, experienced alone, intensely private, pushes itself into our face, but we have only ourselves to hold responsible for willfully looking, for experiencing the image. Do we welcome it, merge it into our own experience? Do we lose ourselves, and then find new responses in ourselves, in looking? Or do we push it away? As in Cage's music and Barker's and Foreman's theatre, I, the individual spectator, hold power over my own experience. The shock of fracture, the silence which denies final meaning, leaves me to pick up the pieces on my own.

And in a sense it answers an age-old question, and reifies the power of the viewer's imagination, opening freedoms available only to the human being. (The lamp the woman holds is an offer of light, shining upon her, inviting us to gaze on her open body. We decide what we experience in looking: shame, guilt, desire, lust, love. What would two people, lovers, see? That, perhaps, is where the performative arts, music, dance and theatre, can also enter.) A falling tree in an unpopulated forest does indeed make a sound, if I can imagine it doing so.

§ 35

The artist impoverishes himself to see with just how little he can express, what remains after what is superfluous has been shorn. In this impoverishment is his commonality with his audience: to find the means of exploration with what is left: the least embellished, the most universal. (Any embellishment a necessary embellishment: the grace notes that bring grace.) How close to darkness and silence one can approach, to leave a mark, a "stain upon the silence." Greatest strength in greatest poverty. Nobility not in the poverty itself, but within the aesthetic attempt.

§ 36

Time and history drive their nails, their fangs, deep into the present body: Krapp's vision and his dream of the punt, mother and daughter of *Footfalls*, inescapable trauma of *Not I*; the whirlwind of the past that undoes the family of *The Homecoming*, the old men of *No Man's Land*, the trio of *Old Times*. The theatrical past is the personal past for the dramatist, he draws all through his words and unsuccessfully attempts to pin them down, again and again, with the failure of his antecedents in living memory, in some kind of ephemeral present. (All touch and pain is memory of touch and pain; receding, left with desire, that same desire for sensation and the feel of the breath on the skin. This is the dynamic of the theatrical moment, the catastrophe of recognition, the knowledge that all falls dark again at the end of the play, a light which does not call attention to itself remains invisible; a light thrown on the stage is that Apollonian consciousness, it pierces, and only pierces when surrounded by the passive dark.) So then theatre takes on a Proustian significance: recapturing in present moment that which is ever disappeared, ever past. Because unrealizable in quotidian life, only realisable between the covers of a book, or between the curtain that rises, then falls.

Light and dark are the simple antitheses of theatre, along with sound and silence, present and past, the end is ever near and scripted, rehearsed over and over for a useless moment of performance. Revolution lies in the deliberate shaft of light and the deliberate word, sculpted by the dark and silence surrounding them. The light falls on a tortuous moment, the word is dragged from the body in its beatific expression of the spirit that lies within the self. The word, like the light, nestles in the dark and silence for only its so brief moment, before it dissipates.

So simple words, for all. So simple light, for all. Bodied speech and presence are impressions on the mute and empty silence. The project and discipline is to suggest these impressions, in some unfinished (because unfinishable) manner, upon the spectator and the auditor. To express a universality, one returns to these basics: instead of inventing new languages (a heinous project, we're all trapped in our languages), one strips one's language and gesture down to the simplest, most elemental traces. Always *le mot juste*, of course, in its multisyllabic splendor our dictionary is as much a gold mine as our omnidimensional history. But art is a contraction, a laser, not an expansion, a floodlight. The laser cuts in its hot precision. The floodlight cools and comforts, and pretends not to recognize night.

§ 37

Nietzsche identifies music's "cosmic symbolism" and language's "organ and symbol of phenomena" as ultimately irreconcilable, and he is correct in this: but he still sees tragedy arising out of music's cosmic symbolism:

> This whole discussion firmly maintains that, whereas lyric poetry depends utterly on the spirit of music, music itself, in its absolute sovereignty, has no *need* at all of images and concepts but merely *tolerates* them as an accompaniment. Lyric poetry can say

> nothing that was not already contained, in a condition of the most enormous generality and universal validity, within the music which forced the lyric poet to speak in images. For this reason it is impossible for language to exhaust the meaning of music's world-symbolism, because music refers symbolically to the original contradiction and original pain at the heart of the primordial unity, and thus symbolizes a sphere which lies above and beyond all appearance. In relation to that primal being every phenomenon is merely a likeness, which is why *language*, as the organ and symbol of phenomena, can never, under any circumstances, externalize the innermost depths of music; whenever language attempts to imitate music it touches the outer surface of music, whereas the deepest meaning of music, for all the eloquence of lyric poetry, can never be brought even one step closer to us.[27]

These are indications of the sign-systems available to the performing arts, those systems that set them apart from the plastic arts: the sign-system of music, the sign-system of language, and the sign-system of gesture are all irreconcilable, but they are joined in an aesthetic palimpsest that leads to the tragic experience. It wasn't so long ago (just over a century) that music, like theatre, was a live performative art and nothing else. The era of sound recording divorced the sign-system of music from the sign-system of physical presence and gesture that accompanied music, in every live performance.

This separation is pained; music without gesture incomplete. In John Cage's work, the invitation to the performer is a primal invitation to re-embody the movement that leads to the formation of sound and to allow sound to inspire and shape a perform-

---

27 Friedrich Nietzsche, *The Birth of Tragedy and Other Writings*. Edited by Raymond Geuss and Ronald Speirs; translated by Ronald Speirs. New York: Cambridge University Press, 1999, p. 36.

er's gesture that occurs within that sound's decay. Cage's pacing and movements in *Water Walk* are an indispensable part of the performance (not to mention the title) of this piece. Its mere aural experience would be lacking. In recent years many composers have been rediscovering gesture as a primal element in musical performance: the sound a determining and necessary, but not a sufficient, factor in the experience of his work.

The sign-system of language inspires, through the spoken manipulation of that system by the performer, a similar set of movements: therefore, the theatrical moment emerging from the word prior to gesture, but gesture the completion of the tragic word. One might set this as the limit and definition of Nietzsche's differentiation between music and the lyric poet. It may be why tragic drama must fail in recognizing the noumena in a way that remains accessible to tragic music. But only if attempted (and attempted *without compromise*) in tragic drama does the utmost limit of the theatrical possibility emerge.

§ 38

The class that possesses. It's an interesting linguistic trope, this: that Shakespeare's work or any expression can be said to properly belong to any group of people (be they theatre practitioners, or academicians, or critics); or that one can lay siege to an expression, grasp it with both hands, and wrest it from the experience of those who also may lay claim to it. Those who utilize the trope may rationalize or excuse this position by explaining that it's merely a rhetorical device, evidence of stridency, but the choice of rhetorical device reveals the unconscious, unexamined ideology of those who opt to utilize that device in defense of that possession: they are making a property claim: they are capitalists, through and through, who own and use the property they own as they see fit, belittling the claims of others who would like to examine that possession. In possession there is moral right and authority.

The ideology underlying this vocabulary is that of a possessory class, a class that can say an expression is "mine" or "ours": experience as property. It delineates the worldview of those who use such words. And within that trope of possession lies moral, ethical, and value judgments. A Beckett text belongs not properly to the page but to the stage, the argument may run, and stage practitioners should be allowed to utilize or contextualize this text in some romantic notion that in restaging Beckett's words through our own "talent" (if that's what we choose to call it) we are serving the play much more than Beckett himself, or his estate, would have us do. We, as theatre practitioners, are right. Beckett and his estate are wrong. We seize the text and Beckett himself be damned. No longer "his," we call it "ours." We impose that interpretation of Beckett on our audiences: the class that rules over interpretation; the audience our peons, who consume what we tell them is true.

Beckett was as much of a man of the theatre as was Shakespeare; he knew what he was doing, and he knew what he was doing when he included his sparse stage directions as part of the dramatic text: the reader of a play directs this play himself, hears it, sees it, in his own imagination. Dramatists allow their plays to be published so that each individual reader can be his own interpretive artist. Read as literature or staged as literature, the play belongs to no one but the individual who experiences it: not to directors or actors, nor to playwrights alone. But the playwright, as he who arranges the words, is first. *Not I* is not possible as a play until Beckett writes it; *King Lear* not possible as theatre until Shakespeare offers the expression built in words. As the aesthetic experience inheres in the individual auditor or reader, that is where meaning eventually lies, to whom the experience properly "belongs": not the professors, nor the denizens of the rehearsal room, but the individual alone in the study or alone, even when sitting with others, in the dark of a theatre.

§ 39

Blood relations; "We're just a bit of pollution."[28] Family is the locus of the first tragedy; it shall be the locus of the last: the dynamics of the nuclear family, the events and personalities that spin around it, conceal the cancer at its heart. Ultimately family is a blindfold for the original sin, as Sophocles, Shakespeare and Beckett had it, of having been born; in bearing children we step into the role of gods, the unconscious destructive will. (If the original sin is having been born, what does that mean for us, how does that define us, the beings who continue to make and bear children?) The audience and performer in the theatre form a forced family, for the duration of a play: an extended family, we would have it; we prefer to think of each of us as a character in a George S. Kaufman family farce, reconciled at the end. But reconciliation is impossible. Solitude, destruction and loneliness are inescapable. Laughter and ameliorist conceptions of community are fictions in tragedy.

Whether it is blood, or genetics, or sentiment, or health insurance coverage, or common cause that holds a family together,

---

28 Theoretical physicist Lawrence M. Krauss, speaking at a panel on cosmology in Chicago. Cited in Richard Panek, "Dark Energy," *The New York Times*, 11 March 2007.

neither the performer nor the audience can know it truly, except that it is beyond our senses and belongs to the realm of the noumenal. We can guess at the traits of the noumenal, but no more than that. The physical universe itself is beginning to provide evidence of this; science may be reaching its end.

Perhaps science is finally catching up to tragedy. Perhaps our rationalistic stages can be prepared for tragedy again. (If it's possible for a dead delusional theatre which prefers to remain blind to be prepared for tragedy again.) Perhaps, in recognising our delusional condition, we rediscover and begin to recognize the microcosm in the macrocosm again and are freed, no longer prisoners of our self-satisfaction and metaphysical arrogance (embodied performance, because most vital and direct, the most effective avenue of this recognition): our own unfathomable dark energies that hold ourselves and the tragic family together, the dark matter which is our own blood and flesh.

§ 40

Terror of the everyday and the necessity of glamour. The embrace and worship of the everyday tedious and repetitive gesture suggest a hatred, even abhorrence of extremity, of transgression, this hatred and abhorrence born (as most hatreds and abhorrences) of fear: A well-founded fear that these will undermine the security and assurances of the everyday. (Tragedy doesn't provide health insurance.) Never mind that this love of the quotidian is composed of a thin veneer of self-importance and an unwarranted expectation of permanence. The possibilities of experience that extremity and transgression invite are drowned in tedium: the tedium of meaningless repetitive work to no end except that of money and security (there is repetitive work in art, in practice, essential to art's necessary precision, but its end is neither fiscal nor safe). The tedium of possession, again born of fear: new cars and condominiums, things to anchor us more deeply into the phenomenal, the dull but insatiable throb of its everyday desires. In their tedium is our security. For some it is air and water, this security. For some it is a drowning death-in-minimal-life.

Small pleasures, greater pains: nothing like the body in the throes of death and decay: fluids ooze, heads pop from bodies dropped through the gallows' trap door. How self-absorbed, without explanation, the living bodies surrounding those of the dead and dying. Clothed in blue jeans and sneakers. These living bodies adorn their self-hatred with the democratic casual.

Erotic tragedy is a glamorous art. It holds comfort and ease as abominations. It's no wonder that it's so informed by luxurious clothing, robes and well-wrought nets. Clothing fetishizes the body as the body fetishizes the spirit, but the fetish provides access to the signified, which stands beyond the object itself. (Costume has always been more signifying than scenery. The Eros of the mask, mask of the face as costumes mask the body: tragedy is a clothed art.) Lush, beautiful costumes, a couture by definition tailored to the individual body of the performer who wears it. Hence the costume's individual expressivity, hence it contains the self's loneliness and desire for union, its vulnerability reaches for the Other. As far from tedium and the quotidian as can be achieved.

Tragedy is not about sensible shoes. Couture, elegance, glamour are by definition theatrical and presentational of the human body, a rediscovery of the expression of erotic tragedy. The clothed onstage body encourages in the spectator an unclothed exploration offstage, in secret, conspiratorial and intimate; a new self-awareness too in the public world: to render that world too a place of beauty and elegance emerging from the phenomenal self. Instead of, by encouraging that democratic casualness and comfort, murdering the spirit through tedium and trivia that mask only boredom and despair.

§ 41

"*The death of tragedy.*" As if to say, at the beginning of the twenty-first century, that tragedy is no longer necessary? Relevant? Accessible? Possible? As with most "death of ..." tropes, it represents wishful thinking more than anything else. Such phrases make good book or essay titles. The attempt to reinvent the old forms in the guise of the ancients or the Elizabethans falls short (mere archaeology, slapping bright paint on the pain of the ancients and wrapping it in Christmas lights, bringing joy to the childish). Contemporary Americans, it appears, have neither the history nor the vocabulary for it (ideologies of left and right, in seeking the ameliorist heaven on earth, a heaven politicians and ideologues think can be found at the center of hell, can't contain the tragic consciousness), and therefore not the interest. But this is merely appearance. The human craves a recognition of the tragic, the American as human as anyone else. If the theatre does not give it to her, she goes elsewhere. It isn't that the tragic is irrelevant; the theatre is irrelevant. The young and shallow wish for their fun, and they shovel it onto the center of the stage. It reeks of waste.

The place for childlike play in tragedy, to find pleasure in the transgression of cultural and social bonds, to laugh, to have one's breath caught short in pleasure. But this is not the same thing as fun. Fun amuses, is safe, consumerist society and culture keep fun penned in the barricades of its puritan limits. Play, on the other hand, is dangerous: it leaps over the barricades of the allowable. And is [?] therefore liberating. Play is joy, irrational wonder, the laugh that shatters community. Fun finds ironic giggles, trivialization, nothing of the self or identity risked. Fun can be incorporated in the Las Vegas spectacle; it constitutes no threat. The ecstatic cry of play, on the other hand, denies the validity of the mob's wishes. It is purely bodied pleasure, to which tickets can't be sold. Fun is amusement for the Costco shopper. Play places assumptions, conformity of any ideology, at risk.

Of course tragedy is alive. It is alive in the work of Barker, Kane, and Crimp. It is alive in the late work of Beckett, in the sexual tragedies of Harold Pinter. In music: in Feldman, Schoenberg, Vivier. In painting and photography. But not in the Microsoft Word documents of American playwrights in the early twenty-first century, or the stages to which MFA and play development programs grant them entry. The maudlin tragedy of Arthur Miller is not tragedy at all, but melodrama (and certainly no play in it). Tragedy in America has yet to be invented. (Our poets have made a start, but their work remains pagebound.) Its place is the theatre. Rather, its place *was* the theatre. (Perhaps those who would like to integrate television and film into the theatrical experience should admit their professional ambitions and go and work in television and film.) Greece had existed for hundreds of years before it staged its first tragedies; England for 500 years before the birth of Shakespeare. Perhaps one day on these shores. Unless we trivialize ourselves out of existence and bastardize all human possibility into a series of YouTube videos long before then.

§ 42

The wound is real, felt, and deep: it is personal and searing, not merely a rhetorical trope. Amusement and diversion are its killing denials. Tragedy is its acceptance, play its redemptive possibility.

§ 43

Criminal intent. The tragic and the erotic intertwine in the recognition, experience and memory of the sublime that contains and sensually validates death as individual, ecstasy as fusion of individuals, experientially in orgasm and materially in reproduction, fully and entirely aware and deliberate (not to deny the mystery that a single experience contains both). As these are recognitions and not ameliorative, they refuse to serve society, in particular the society's culture industry, which sickens, kills and blackens what it touches. In fact, quite the opposite: the highest tragic and erotic experience in theatre is contained in the expression of its elegant fetishistic criminality, a love in which the audience, as individuals, is invited to conspire.

§ 44

No escape. Even in our greatest pleasures we find the greatest pains, opening our flesh to its fullest sensibility renders us that much more profoundly sensible to the wound that doesn't heal, the heights of our pleasure equal the depths of our suffering. There are those who consider, rightfully, causality as a dull prison rather than as a calculus of practical, pragmatic achievement: an equation without irrational numbers. Prisons are all predictability, dullness, greatest fear in the least uncertainty. Pragmatism seeps into the heart of theatre and gains purchase on its organs of expression, growing like a cancer, spreading from one element to another. But this is a dishonest, unhealthy wound. It is a wound which finds its motivation in its dull nature, instead of a wound self-inflicted, motivated by the necessity to discover. Alternatively: in that deep pain the greatest, most rewarding pleasure, until the two commingle and it's hard to say which is which. American pragmatism, as it inflicts its own wounds, approaches all wounds as of the same nature (and believes that an antibacterial salve and a band-aid will suffice to heal), pessimism perceived as a disease of the mind and spirit, whereas it is recognition, which lacks cure. What is seen cannot be unseen. Suffering and pleasure of which we are capable remain with us as ghosts and ambitions of the psyche. In art, we reach.

§ 45

On reading Howard Barker's Gertrude*: statements of intent.* There are practical outcomes and effects in approaching theatre as sensual lyricism, one such effect a growing realization of contemporary theatre's death (and not a tragic death that contemplates the ends of ecstasy and the decay of the body, but a psychic death of numbed, anesthetized nerve endings and cold shallow eyes of glass). Death inhering in unquestioning acceptance of the falsehoods of meaning-bearing mainstream narrative (instead of the discrete event or the event of language itself), meaning-bearing mainstream character (what a lie, this superficially-possessed idea of integrated character; our lives don't have character arcs over time, the pretense that they do another nail in the coffin of our ability to exist; we constantly change, "growth" is a value judgment that dismisses the elemental; how can we have a significant theatre that lies to us like this? We so intently kill the possibilities of experience with interpretation). Some plays, the few plays that can possibly reify the theatre as a life-giving force, are unapproachable except as music, performers and composers without self to filter language, sensibility, sensuality.

I no longer ever ask questions about meaning aloud, questions about meaning invite that hideously vapid death. René Char: "No bird has the heart to sing in a thicket of questions." Especially the question, "What does it mean?" Which is attempted homicide and should be prosecuted and punished as such.

I would prefer (playwright as composer) not untrained performers but performers trained as musicians (actress and actor as joined with instrument, that instrument the body, speaking, as musical instruments are beautiful and profoundly integral and sovereign in their histories and construction when silent but most beautiful when sounded); as with soloists or chamber ensembles, the director or conductor utterly unnecessary; the text itself director enough, the score itself conductor enough. (Directors are meaning-makers, conductors perhaps not so much because their music more physiologically supple.) This lays a heavier burden on us all. But unless we burden ourselves with these imperatives our worlds remain unshattered. Effect lies in study and discipline; is there life otherwise?

A continual, renewed recognition of the need for secret conspiracies, among spiritual co-conspirators, in darkened rooms. This is also as political as it sounds.

§ 46

"The artistic tendency is not expansive, but a contraction."[29] Beckett's "principle of parsimony" restricts expression to the smallest gestures in the most confined spaces, for all the broad expanses of the landscape it is still the interior of a skull. The artist chooses between the encyclopedic *Finnegans Wake* and the muck-under-the-microscope of *How It Is*.

It seems clear that Joyce's early imprecation to the artist—that she must choose "silence, exile and cunning" in Stephen Dedalus' classic formulation—is a failure. (In all fairness to Joyce, it must be said that he too, in maturity, recognized it as a failure.) All movement is within, through the veins and arteries, very real flesh and blood, of the self. No exile provides comfort, no cunning enough to trick the will. She swallows, she absorbs the world, lest she be swallowed and absorbed by it. In the erasure of the line between subject and object, she can't objectify through escape from the shores, but maps inwardly, to find affinities and affordances, other selves and objects and events with which she can join and thereby produce and express, to become fertilized by them, to give birth. "Silence, exile and cunning" still accepts the dichotomy, defines one by violent opposition to the landscape, rejection of it. Better to offer, and disappear into, silence, time and solitude (these perhaps the only principles worth fighting and dying for), violence not in opposition and separation but in union and integration.

29 Samuel Beckett, *Proust*, in *The Poems, Short Fiction and Criticism of Samuel Beckett*. Edited by Paul Auster. New York: Grove Press, 2006, p.539.

§ 47

United Colors of Benetton. A cry for more customers, this, the talk of diversity in the consumerist age. The theatre's leadership, artistic practitioners and audience should reflect the demographic of the modern multicultural democratic state, goes the valorous idea (and raising the question, "When is a quota not a quota?"); but after decades of labels—Black Theatre, Queer Theatre, Women's Theatre—and the slow but undoubted inclusion of these tropes in the mainstream theatre, do we have a theatre that has somehow eradicated or even alleviated injustice, any more than we have a culture that has done so? Or has injustice simply driven itself deeper underground, to emerge in the gross perversions of the smiling progressive state, which continues to send agents of violence to far-off lands? The stages have changed and made room for these new tropes, but has the theatre become any more necessary—or necessary at all—as a result? Or do we simply propose a Benetton advertisement as the ideal mirror of the theatre's audience and creative and administrative communities, selling images of multicultural contentment (married to a grinning or pouting youth which denies maturity), as well as the desiccated products of the corporation behind the advertisement?

Such a theatre cannot survive—its mere economic inefficiency will see to that. Nor should it, for then it becomes merely another instrument of discouragement, a monolith of self-congratulatory contentment that presence expresses all. It is not necessary. Howard Barker suggests what kind of theatre may indeed be necessary, but that necessity must be recaptured:

> Theatre is no longer capable of entertainment, despite its continual degeneration into the *realm* of entertainment. It is no lon-

ger possible to make it product, despite being part of mechanistic production processes [...] and it is *perfectly inefficient*, the worst nightmare of accountancy. That is its profound redemption. In comparison with technological forms, information-systems, the capitalization of education, the relentless flow of life-imitation and fantasy available on television and film, it asserts its problematic nature and resists incorporation by its very *form*. And beyond this ... wherever theatre offers itself as entertainment it reveals itself as *degradation* even in the eyes and ears of unknowing audiences who desert the theatre and continue to desert it the more slavishly theatre attempts to win them by catering for its perceived taste. Another triumph of human nature over the market. Another triumph of the soul over the ethics of pleasure. Precisely because such a theatre is audience-led it is doomed to extinction. The demise of such a theatre should be welcomed as the peace of death gives welcome relief to an incurably suffering man. We assert the contrary practice. The theatre which is to be *necessity* repudiates the audience as the gratifying principle of production. It exists for itself, and paradoxically, by existing for itself it becomes a necessity for an audience for the reason that men and women ache for the representation of tragedy—which is pain—and this secret longing for the *incomprehensible nature of pain*—is beyond politics, beyond social order, and beyond conscience. It is *instinct*. Incomprehensible pain—the ignorant text—is loathed by society as society loathes instinct itself; society has an institutional investment in the eradication of pain and the elimination of tragedy from the sphere of art. Tragedy is inherently irrational, it affirms the *limits of social action* and therefore is fundamentally immune to the propaganda of the state and the revolution alike. It is no surprise then, that in an age of ideology and welfare the conventional dominant forms of popular theatre have been comic or musical, and no wonder that governments and their allies in the leisure industry have tried to smear tragedy as "pessimistic" and "elitist

..." two terms we would be wise to adopt, cherish and advertize.[30]

§ 48

O'Neill's radicalism. With his late plays Eugene O'Neill burrows through realism and the Expressionist stage to come out upon a darker landscape: significance and meaning are shattered. The drunks in the back room of Harry Hope's bar in *The Iceman Cometh* are exaggerations of the audience as collective: sharers not in individual pipedreams but within the cultural construct of ameliorist and personal illusion (literally so in the character of anarchist Hugo Kalmar). Hickey the dramatist/salesman expresses his shattering experience in talking, constant talking, a thrashing against his experience's own lack of utilitarian meaning. Hickey's secret is the pain and violence of action based in love. His effort to draw the drunks back into the light again, as the dramatist tries to draw the audience into blinding recognition, is doomed to failure: years of illusion have condemned them to failure, however jolly their retreat into drunkenness, or the culture, may appear. But Hickey knows, as do the individuals Don Parrit and Larry Slade; Slade is embedded in this culture, too much of a coward himself to dare action, Parrit through suicide seeks his way out. (Hickey is a skilled salesman and marketer: he sells happiness to his wife; her gain is her death; she "sleeps with" the iceman, who comes; his profit is his arrogant so-called truth. He should have been a marketing consultant in the theatre.)

---

30 Howard Barker, *Arguments for a Theatre*. Third edition. Manchester, England: Manchester University Press, 1997, pp. 144-145.

Retreat is denied to the Tyrones in *Long Day's Journey into Night*, the great dream play that anatomizes the cancer at the center of the Tyrone family and at the center of the theatre. Tyrone, an actor, offers Mary a theatre of family and affection as much as an anesthetic of experience as her morphine dreams. Her own sexuality has produced three children; the two who survive shore up the house as the decay continues within. At the final curtain, in her wedding dress, she denies the experience that began with Tyrone's love, seeking virginity again. It is unrecoverable, of course, but her illusion holds her husband and children wrapped, and rapt, in her dream, even as they remain torn, bleeding and dying.

Duration is the avenue of revelation: these are high masses that require more than three hours (more than four hours, in the case of *The Iceman Cometh*) for their uncut production; three times the length of most contemporary American plays. But these are surgeries that can't be performed sloppily: language and performance are scalpels, not machetes. O'Neill sent the audience not into the late evening for a drink or dinner or the post-show panel discussion, but into a world past midnight: into the black morning, without appeal.

§ 49

Internal memorandum. An official government organ of either propaganda or censorship is unnecessary when individuals have so thoroughly internalized the assumptions of an ideology, moral dogma, government or culture industry that they will give up individual autonomy for the unquestioning furtherance of an abstract goal defined by those organs. What need for propaganda when the artist will without external compulsion do the same work in support of an ideology, or will censor himself and repress his doubts as irrelevant? Especially if his aesthetic goals are those lauded by the culture industry—entertainment, self-aggrandizement, a wan sentimental pity, or education, to name only four examples—as a means to the absorption of individual agency into collective response. The play that does not entertain (in the narrowest of definitions of that word) or educate, that sees through the transparent ease of sentimental pity, that refuses to self-promote one's careerist agenda, denies that absorption, throwing the individual spectator upon his own powers of imagination or speculation, both of which are threats to ideological assumptions.

It is a truism of the progressive collectivist that the "individual" himself is a mere historical and social construct; so the collectivist will be expected to say, and it is valid insofar as the individual will bear within him certain traits or beliefs, certain common knowledge, lent by collective experience. But this is only a partial answer that does not account for the complexity of human experience within and without the community, nor does it validate the sufficiency of those collective beliefs. The tragedies of *Oedipus* and *King Lear* lie in the fracture between collective cultural abstractions (fatherhood, justice, matrimony, kingship) and the individual autonomous self. There are two avenues to freedom: resignation and repudiation. Neither are necessarily "happy" in the sense that American culture is a pursuit of happiness. But they deny the stupor of the collective and embrace the possibility of imagination and ecstasy in the process of that contemplative resignation or repudiation. (Imagine Oedipus unpunished by himself or Creon ...)

In the culture industry, freedom of choice is the cereal aisle of the supermarket, the 800 channels of cable television or the hundreds of offerings of performances in New York theatrical circles. For the autonomous individual, freedom of choice is in choosing to refuse what the culture industry offers, and to imagine something other, to put the individual secret on stage ...

Their collective ideologies are embodied too, and they set that decaying fluorescent flesh to laughing and dancing, crying and moping, and dig their hands deep into those bodies ...

§ 50

Resignation and repudiation. Resignation provides no impulse or energy for the aesthetic effort; repudiation does. Resignation is the final acceptance of the solitude in which the radical speculator in moral, ethical and aesthetic conundrums eventually finds himself, but in reaching this knowledge it is necessary for the will to be in conflict with itself: it is the will which writes and performs, with inevitable conflict against the culture and ideology which it repudiates (and which also exemplifies the will in the phenomenal arena). Resignation is the condition of will-less solitude; repudiation the road, the dynamic that leads there. This is not merely the status of the Romantic, but of the tragic especially. It is the status of Oedipus at the end of Sophoclean tragedy, in which the same conflict can be found in the *Philoctetes*, and why he is the greater tragedian than Aeschylus, whose *Oresteia* ends in reconciliation.

In the theatre, the spoken word and the body are the agents of this repudiation, and as it repudiates the desiccated phenomenal consciousness it welcomes a new consciousness through ecstasy and the recognition of mortality. Hence the erotic, the internal knowledge of the body's decay, the dead. If repudiation is in the service of this new knowledge, the word and the body conduct this repudiation in transgression and new experience, ever at risk of loss. "When I am asked where then is to be found the *most intimate knowledge* of that inner essence of the world, of that thing-in-itself which I have called *the will-to-live*; or where is one most clearly aware of that essence; or where does it attain the most positive revelation of itself,—then I must point to *voluptuousness in the act of copulation*. ... This is the true essence and core of all things, the aim and purpose of all existence. Therefore it is also for living beings *subjectively* the aim of all their actions, their highest gain; and *objectively* it is that which keeps the world going, for the inorganic world is attached to the organic through knowledge."[31] (When he wrote this, Schopenhauer was the lover of Caroline Richter, an actress: an agent of self-reinvention.)

It is a copulation in both word and deed, in which desire flows through both word and body: it is theatrical and dramatic in its prime motivation. Once theatre and drama are discovered as revelations of this, a revelation gained only through repudiation, it is a wonder that there is so much theatre, so much drama, created today. Given the sublimity of the tragic theatrical act, who would want to make, or to witness, any theatre other than this?

§ 51

Risk and the theatre of fear. Fear justifies the surveillance state (perhaps we shall call this "transparency," which reflects more positively upon us). As men and women internalize and rationalize the constant state of fear as pragmatism or practicality, it is

---

31 Arthur Schopenhauer, *Manuscript Remains: Volume III*. Translated by E.F.J. Payne. New York: Berg Publishers, 1988, pp. 262-263.

no longer recognized as fear. Instead, the giving-up of the private sphere to digitalization and surveillance—as the entire world becomes a panopticon in the interest of an illusory safety—drives the truth of the night to become subterranean and even more conspiratorial than it already was. We pretend to no secrets or ulterior motives, but this pretense is hypocritical. Our fears have become so ingrained into our daily experience and behaviors that we no longer characterize them as fears. Instead of examining and exploring the dark corners of our experience, we pretend that they do not exist. The growth of the cancer is palpable.

There has always been a close relationship between fear and risk: where we are afraid, we do not risk the expression of a personal truth; and, as with the surveillance state, we rationalize this safer expression as pragmatism or practicality. For there is much at risk. A denial of critical, professional or academic preferment; the horror of penury (the greatest, perhaps, in both of the post-capitalist geopolitical and personal spheres); similarly, the increasing difficulty of securing the wherewithal to produce the work one envisions; the fear of being thought intellectual and cold; the fear of allying oneself with the abject or the ridiculed; the terror of the communitarian, solitary, with silence as his only companion; the suspicion that there will be no compensatory laugh to undermine the tragic recognition; and, of course, one wants to be well-liked and fears the disapproval of the community. Risky behavior becomes suspect in the panopticon, subject to scrutiny, ridicule and punishment. And yet, what deeper experience and recognition can explore our entire condition if we do not take those risks? And what kind of art will be produced if, so tentative and frightened in merely our discussions of theatre, we are—and why shouldn't we expect this, given our fearful behavior and expression in the public arena—similarly tentative and frightened in the theatre we produce (*ex cathedra*, as it were)? There is no safe harbor nor room for fear in the tragic theatre that genuinely speculates in both form and content (assuming that these can be spoken of independently, an assumption that must be rejected if an art is to live). It risks everything for the recognitions and ecstasies that pain and pleasure contemplated in darkness with others can produce. It gains everything worth gaining as human beings as well.

§ 52

Play of thought. Every play is the expression of a single thought whose tentacles extend to enwrap dramatist, performer and spectator in the necessity of its expression. As Schopenhauer's most significant nearly thousand-page work too is described by its author as the expression of "a single thought,"[32] this thought is not simple but extends through ontology, phenomenology, aesthetics and metaphysics. It does not beg forgiveness for its complexity. And it is a thought, as Adorno describes, which is true in that it fails to understand itself. Expression and speculation, not elucidation or understanding, are at the center of the effort. It refuses the judgment of the reviewer's pen and finds its significance in its saying, reveling in its prolixity and lyricism, as the mouth wraps itself around the sounds of the word. It remains without closure but provides possibility in the solitude of the figures who remain in the theatrescape at the curtain.

Because the tragic or catastrophic thought (a thought suggested by the originary impulse of the dramatist—and here

---

32 Arthur Schopenhauer, *The World as Will and Representation: Volume I.* Translated by E.F.J. Payne. New York: Dover Publications, 1966, p. xii.

"thought" must be conceived as not mere intellectuation but as a spiritual, emotional, religious and physical impulse as well) defies the administered culture in its refusal to concede to that culture the defeat and erasure of the individual, it remains abject to that culture, the target of ridicule or deliberate silence, the elephant that remains in the room. The performers, designers, audience participate in the tragic thought in the moment of performance, urged forth from the dramatist's words: that performance therefore remains a crime, the dramatist the mastermind perhaps but the other collaborators equal accomplices in its commission. Which is why tragic and catastrophic theatre, why this single thought, remains conspiracy and secret, private, a citizen of the dark. Because certainly bodied, certainly thought, of its time and place and by deliberate intent simultaneously exiled from it. A criminal act, and in criminality it becomes *erotic* ...

§ 53

Being modern. However postmodernism may be defined, it is clearly considered by its theorists to be subsequent to the Modernist period at least in time. But more than that, postmodernism is a reaction (a progressive reaction, according to its enthusiasts) against the tenets of the Modernist movement, tenets that arose from the need for a radical individualism, mythic, tragic and urban, recognized from within the conditions existing in the latter half of the nineteenth century. Sociologist Georg Simmel noted, "The deepest problems of modern life derive from the claim of the individual to preserve the autonomy and individuality of his existence in the face of overwhelming social forces, of historical heritage, of external culture, and of the technique of life."[33] It also self-consciously married form to content, and, through this metaphor, individual body to spirit, as inseparable. While Modernism suffered its greatest challenges through the two world wars of the early twentieth century, these wars also lent validity to Modernism's central assumptions: that the comprehensive worldview offered by the Enlightenment could not forestall catastrophe, a conclusion that the Modernists had suspected for years. In response the postmodern mind turned from this conclusion and posited the body (shorn of spirit, which was either non-existent or as irrelevant as a personal god) as merely another image in a world of mass-produced images: postmodernism as a cowardly escape, however much fun it might be. Here the individual was a mere construct of social forces and the images that surrounded him, lacking autonomy and discouraging imagination. The self and the art product were culturally-produced palimpsests, nothing more nor less. In this sense postmodernism exhibited an even more dulling pessimism than it charged Modernism with: the "nothing to be done" that kept Vladimir and Estragon waiting for Godot, for if the individual was a mere construct, why not surrender to the Culture Industry and the institutions comprising it? (Beckett himself did "do something," writing plays, prose and poetry that examined and critiqued this condition.)

Though Modernism as a literary movement may be considered anachronistic, it is not for that reason invalid, and it may continue to give courage. In the theatre, some are seizing the Modernist perspective again in response to the postmodern

---

33 Georg Simmel, *The Sociology of Georg Simmel*. Translated by Kurt H. Wolff. New York: The Free Press, 1950, p. 409.

mashup, the latter relevant to culture perhaps but irrelevant to the autonomous self, a warm and comforting blanket in which to wrap fear and trembling. At a 2009 Howard Barker conference in Wales, Elisabeth Angel-Perez's keynote speech was titled "Reinventing Grand Narratives: Barker's Challenge to Postmodernism," intimating that the broad historical and philosophical canvases of the Modernist project continue to be an antagonistic response to postmodernism. This is not to suggest that Barker considers himself a Modernist; this I don't know; but his favorite philosopher, Theodor Adorno, has the reputation of defending Modernism against the encroachment of the postmodernist Culture Industry. A Modernist theatre may partake of the formal explosions of musical modernists Schoenberg and Webern early in the twentieth century. In 1938, Adorno wrote, "The terror which Schoenberg and Webern spread, today as in the past, comes not from their incomprehensibility but from the fact that they are all too correctly understood. Their music gives form to that anxiety, that terror, that insight into the catastrophic situation which others merely evade by regressing. They are called individualists, and yet their work is nothing but a single dialogue with the powers which destroy individuality—powers whose 'formless shadows' fall gigantically on their music. In music, too, [*and just as much in contemporary theatre—GH*] collective powers are liquidating an individuality past saving, but against them only individuals are capable of consciously representing the aims of collectivity."[34] This was prior to Hiroshima and Auschwitz, which still loomed as formless shadows over Asia, Europe and the modern world. The world remains just as modern.

---

34 Theodor W. Adorno, *The Culture Industry: Selected Essays on Mass Culture*. New York: Routledge Classics, 2001, p. 60.

§ 54

Of the spirit. The Christian conception of fleshed word as a means of access to spirit (through the bodied god, his sacrifice, rituals such as the Eucharist in which flesh is taken into flesh; though Christianity is not alone in this conception, it is among the most recent Western exemplars) finds unique aesthetic equivalence in theatre. Here the actor and dramatist explore these roads to access, as does a musical performer, who allows a musical composition to pass through her body (without the body, even that of the synthesizer operator or the composer in a recording studio, unheard), sacrificing its cultural and social position to the aesthetic position: an offering to the individual audience member, which differentiates aesthetic performance from the organized church. The physical and perhaps emotional discomfort and suffering of the performer in a Beckett or Kane play is an act of sacrifice offered up to the individual auditor, who may be expected to either share in it, contemplate it, or find offense in it: the discomfort and suffering transcended in the grace of its performance towards a spiritual end. Instead, however, of these ecstasies offered to god and to the witnessing of fellow celebrants (for the church audience is well-lit, the theatrical audience shrouded in darkness), they are instead offered to a communion of individual spirits, if such can be said to exist within the phenomenal world. Each dramatic text and musical score, unlike a poem or a recording, is a liturgy which contains the means to that higher consciousness, but is not an end in itself, which does not demonstrate its power until its performance. It is then no wonder that churches debate the content and wording of their liturgies for decades before approving them for use in the church, for words demonstrate power if they do not contain that power fully within themselves. The priesthood knew this, the governing hierarchies of the organized church retain the power for approbation within themselves, knowing what is at stake in words and sounds. The dramatist without a stage, or a composer without a performer, creators without performative collaborators, remain hermetic, which has its value, but it is not that of the theatre. The *erotics* of performance requires partnership if it isn't to remain masturbation ...

§ 55

Schopenhauer, Freud, Lacan. In the index to the Standard Edition of Freud's work, references to Schopenhauer and Nietzsche occur relatively frequently, Hegel only once. This is not to deny, however, that the Hegelian concept of dialectic is relevant, especially towards Freud's later, more pessimistic conceptions of the duel between the Thanatonic and Erotic drives. If Lacan therefore goes back to Freud (as he conceived his project), the Hegelian conception of history is a palimpsest upon the construct of Schopenhauer's subject. Although Schopenhauer's subject is "an eye that cannot see itself," it can nonetheless know itself: "the world is the self-knowledge of the will," he said in the *Manuscript Remains*. Tragedy is not only means but end to this self-knowledge.

That said, one can reject Schopenhauer's resignation or quietude as insufficient, especially when it pertains to aesthetic creation, without rejecting the metaphysics that lie beneath both Schopenhauer and Freud. Aesthetic creation is an act of will, or self-creation, and impossible within resignation and quietude. So the struggle or desire continues, necessarily willed in both senses.

But does Hegel's dialectic necessarily lead to progress—that is, to some form of synthesis, to some end of reconciliation and therefore some amelioration of suffering? In Barker's *The Europeans*, Ludwig names Katrin's baby "Concilia," an attempt to provide some closure or absorption, some possession of Katrin's suffering in her rape by the Turks and her ensuing childbirth, for the furtherance of the state's peace; at the end of the play, she finds freedom for expression of her pain (and therefore love of Starhemberg) only when she and Starhemberg surrender the child to the Turks: surrendering Concilia to the former enemy. The construction of the self, of the subject, is never complete but only finds full expression when conciliation is rejected—or, more precisely, surrendered as a possibility of closure or amelioration of suffering; when both pain and pleasure remain possessions of the individual rather than the state.

Barker's is a third way between Schopenhauer's and Hegel's construction of the subject: the subject must abandon any sense of resignation or synthesis, any certitude, for freedom. (Hegel: "In a true tragedy, both parties must be right." But "right" is both a logical and a moral judgment, and moral speculation forecloses any such final judgment.) Both Katrin and Starhemberg accept the origin; they accept beginning in the body. And Lacan's *jouissance* begins with the baby recognizing its own complete body in a mirror: a full recognition, rather than one of fragmented parts: when all that is hidden and seemingly disconnected becomes whole. It is the origin of the obligation to express: this is the journey itself.

§ 56

"I don't go to the theatre." If an art form is to thrive it must feed a spiritual hunger. It's not enough and has never been enough simply to point to descriptions of theatre ("I can take any empty space and call it a bare stage. A man walks across this space whilst someone else is watching, and this is all that is needed for an act of theatre to be engaged,"[35] for example) and expect audiences to flock gratefully to the auditorium or, for that matter, any site designated as a space for theatrical performance. There is nothing special or magical about it and is besides insulting in its condescension. It demonstrates moreover a lack of respect for those who see nothing in the contemporary theatre that attracts them. "Theatre" itself is not corrupt or dying and doesn't need to be saved. An incomplete list of New York productions in any given week numbers nearly 100, if not more. (There are, I believe, many fewer Hollywood and independent films currently in release.) It is not those who attend these shows who matter, but those who do not.

All of the marketing in the world, viral or otherwise, will not serve to generate spectators if the spectators find nothing there, nothing in the YouTube trailers or the Facebook "events" invitations or the postcard, that suggests that the theatre offers them something that the rest of the culture industry does not, and for much less money. If they see a theatre they want, they will pay for it, as they pay for luxury items of greater or lesser price.

The necessity is not material but spiritual, and what lacks in the culture industry is an arena for moral and imaginative speculation. It lacks poetry (verse it has in abundance) and tragedy

---

35 Peter Brook, *The Empty Space*. New York: Touchstone Books, ADD YEAR, p. 9.

(melodrama too is not absent). It lacks the genuinely radical and revolutionary possibility of new perception, perceptions that have been neither generated nor absorbed by the culture industry already, perceptions which are not controlled by a creative but authoritarian consciousness that imposes meaning and significance on events rather than freeing the spectator's consciousness to explore his or her own. (This is why it remains, and should remain, elitist. One spectator is enough.)

Theatre's going nowhere; it will always be with us, and it already has its audience. But the new audience will not attend unless it sees theatre as a source for spiritual and speculative sustenance: they do not see it this way now, and contemporary theatre seems happy to feed itself whatever it likes. There will always be customers for McDonald's.

§ 57

> These works are a series of acts best comprehended in groups or as a continuity. Except as a created revelation, a new experience, they are without value. It is my desire that they be kept in groups as much as possible and remain so. ... So I am in the strange position of seeking an environment for the work and the small means wherein I'll be free to continue the "act."[36]

Houston's Rothko Chapel is a small unremarkable building set just off a suburban corner, adjoining a series of plain, low houses and a college campus. Within it, however, is a world entirely itself, as real as the houses and classrooms surrounding it but an enclosure of myth and tragedy. The 14 maroon-and-black can-

---

36 Clyfford Still to Betty Parsons in a 1949 letter. Cited in Susan J. Barnes, *The Rothko Chapel: An Act of Faith*. Houston, TX: The Rothko Chapel, 1996, p. 26.

vases inside invite absorption into the space, originally designed by Philip Johnson, dedicated to their exhibition. Famously non-representative, they achieve the distillation of myth and tragedy in the sense that Nietzsche wrote in *The Birth of Tragedy*, the book that of all Nietzsche's work was most influenced by Schopenhauer:

> But where the subject is an artist, it is already released and redeemed from the individual will and has become, as it were, a medium, the channel through which the one truly existing subject celebrates its release and redemption in semblance. ... Only insofar as the genius, during the act of artistic procreation, merges fully with that original artist of the world does he know anything of the eternal essence of art; for in this condition he resembles, miraculously, that uncanny image of fairy-tale which can turn its eyes around and look at itself; now he is at one and the same time subject and object, simultaneously poet, actor, and spectator.[37]

Within this chapel, and within the bodies of work by artists such as Wagner, Syberberg, Beckett, Feldman, Rothko and Barker, we find a new definition for the tragic epic. Ordinarily the word "epic" is treated as genre, or formal description, but more precisely it is *the representation of the will's noumenal cosmology through phenomenal means*. In this sense "epic" ties Homer's poems to Beckett's. As a cosmology the body of work is necessarily precise and detailed, requiring more than a mere story or anecdote—or a single painting—for its full expression. It requires that imaginative extension besides.

---

37 Nietzsche, *op. cit.*, pp. 32-33.

Lest we balk at the word "tragedy" itself as mere genre, let us consider it here as a dynamic, a consciousness, a perspective, rather than a form. The epic artist insists upon tragedy's expression through lengthy duration in time and expansive extension in space. (Leaving aside for the moment the idea of "comic epics," which will have far more numerous defenders, unlike the tragic epic, which in post-capitalism, unsellable, stands alone.) In terms of duration and space, the expression is extensive. Wagner's *Ring* and *Tristan und Isolde*; Syberberg's seven-hour-plus *Hitler: A Film from Germany*; the four hours of Beckett's dramatic output after 1962 (these small plays like canvases; arranged in a group, they display as epic a vision as Rothko's Chapel); Barker's day-long *The Ecstatic Bible* and other plays. The extension through time is deliberate. The description of cosmology, especially as an aesthetic project, necessitates time and patience.

Extension through space may be another matter. As impressive as it is, the Rothko Chapel is not a large building. In a letter to Dominique de Menil, Mrs. Gifford Phillips reported on a conversation she had with Rothko: that Rothko had described to her his project of one-man museums in "small, very simple buildings—made of cinderblock, I remember that—scattered throughout the country in small towns. And each building would be an homage to a particular artist. One would contain Reinhardts, one Rothkos ..."[38] The size of the arena seems to be unimportant; what is essential is that the work seem to *possess* the space entire, to blend with it: to express that all-encompassing cosmos.

Perhaps the root of my affection for small spaces, studio theatres of only 50 seats or so, lies in the ability of the work to more easily possess a small space than a large one. The epic artist lays

---

38 Cited in Barnes, *op cit.*, p. 26.

siege not only to contemporary consciousness but to environment as well. Barker's *exordia*, the preliminary *mise-en-scène* which he presents to the audience entering the performance space, is a means of possessing that space, of breaking the continuity between foyer and playing area. The foyer to the Rothko Chapel is plain and functional. (As is the foyer to the theatre possessed by that other epic artist, Richard Foreman, who spent the last few decades working in a similarly small space, smaller than Rothko's Chapel; Foreman also presented a stage picture to the audience as they enter, a sculpture of objects and setting that the audience can begin to explore.) Syberberg's sole setting is a soundstage; bereft of exteriors, the film takes place in a world as self-contained as the crystal ball containing Edison's Black Maria that forms a motif to the *Hitler* film.

These artists invite us in to these cosmologies, these worlds. In the case of Rothko's Chapel, these cosmologies are shorn of traditional figuration to reveal the essence of tragedy: beyond names and story (so many artists make the mistake of thinking that a mere recycling of a story or the use of a name like Oedipus is a means of confronting the tragedies that lay behind these stories and figures; these artists lay claim to them in a desperate attempt to lend their own work significance), but inherent in the very real instruments of the art form: the pigment, the canvas, the body, the sound. The substance lies in the real, the world of the phenomenon. Rothko warns of this fetishization of story and name:

> If our titles recall the known myths of antiquity, we have used them again because they are the eternal symbols upon which we must fall back to express basic psychological ideas. They are the symbols of man's primitive fears and motivations, no matter in

> which land or what time, changing only in detail but never in substance. ...
>
> Our presentation of these myths however must be in our own terms which are at once more primitive and more modern than the myths themselves. ... The myth holds us, therefore, not thru its romantic flavor, not thru [*sic*] the remembrance of the beauty of some by gone age, not thru [*sic*] the possibilities of fantasy, but because it expresses to us something real and existing in ourselves, as it was to those who first stumbled upon the symbols to give them life.[39]

In his late work, Rothko's titles too were shorn of mythic resonance, often mere descriptions of the colors within the painting. But he still insisted upon the tragic resonance. And his work was prone to the same kinds of misunderstandings as Beckett's. Once, an observer called Rothko's canvases of bright yellows and oranges "celebrations." Rothko responded that these colors, to him, were the colors of an inferno.[40]

The contemporary epic, tragic vision is rare. The comic can be sold; everybody likes to laugh and have a good time. But the more lacerating self-scrutiny that tragedy invites is of a different nature and inheres in this cosmology: in the imaginative creation of a world like the Rothko Chapel, of a space in which we can feel those things that have remained foreign or hidden to us in the spaces outside the chapel or the theatre. What emerges is not some vague abstract sense of hope or happiness, but the sense of life's possibilities: ecstasy in recognition. On my first visit to the chapel I carried in my arms my new daughter, far too young

---

39 Mark Rothko, interview, "The Portrait and the Modern Artist," WNYC radio, October 13, 1943.

40 Mark Rothko to Arnold Glimcher. Cited in Barnes, *op. cit.*, p. 23.

to know where she was or why she was there; she will not remember this visit. But I hope (with a true, fleshed, real hope born of that recognition) that, when she's older, she will vaguely sense that, one day early in her life, she experienced those canvases, that silence, that dim light. And that early in her life she will have experienced, will have been given access to, will have been encouraged to seek out such consecrated aesthetic spaces that give her entry into her own unexpected imagination of the world.

§ 58

His canvases, Rothko insisted, were tragic: he never accepted the opinions of those who characterized them as calm, or without conflict. Peering closer at them (as he would have us look at them—from eighteen inches away, he said in his more dogmatic moments), we see the drama within the light. Color was not the subject of his work, but light itself. The drama and the tragedy lay were in the fading of the color: where blues became black, or yellows white. Here were the violent scrapings of the imagination, the attacks, the brushstrokes or paintdrips that marred these seemingly calm works, that robbed them of that very stillness that many viewers championed. Here too were the negative spaces that surrounded Giacometti's sculptures, or the silences that formed the profound ground of Feldman's music. Giacometti's wire, Feldman's attacks, were excuses for the fadings of space and silence that they left behind: Beckett's "literature of the unword" writ in light and sound.

Like Shakespeare. For what is *Hamlet* or *King Lear* but the elucidation of that vibrating—ultimately fading—energy between act and thought, word and silence, identity and self? In this context, questions of either hope or hopelessness become laughable. This is not the dramatist's dilemma, but that of the simpleton, who in his simplicity reduces all to simple moralistic goods and evils. (When we ask whether or not Lear or Hamlet are responsible for what happens to them, we put our own prejudice and compassion and ignorance, not the characters, in the dock.) Shakespeare offers neither optimism nor pessimism, hope nor hopelessness. And his offerings are beyond the call of mere 12-year-olds, who in all their purity remain unconflicted and pristinely ignorant. (Shall we valorize childhood and its vaunted if theoretical innocence as a special interest? Fine. Then what of adulthood, and experience? Or are these all lies, the past discarded as a toy with which we've grown tired or found embarrassing?)

In the bodied art of theatre those grays and near-silences are the arenas of eroticism, of idiosyncratic sensation and sensuality. Shades of man/woman, masculine/feminine, dominant/submissive, sadist/masochist (like act/thought, word/silence, identity/self, if not identical to them), not dichotomies but spectra along the lines of which you play—play as necessary risk. You touch me somehow; the memory on my flesh lingers. I have it in my memory and it lasts, it can't be denied. This memory is the product of age, not youth. This comes only with time and is not the product of a review or feature story. (These are only of the day, not of the life.) This sensation and sensuality are far from a cause of celebration. That they contain the ecstatic is not an invitation to a party that lends self-congratulation to men and women. It is instead an invitation that leads to a contemplation of the distance and death that it also contains, a death of self and certainty in the midst of the orgasmic loss of self. It is also the miraculousness of birth, of which the orgasm is only a first step.

Children's theatre? Today, all our theatre is children's theatre. I suspect that the task is not to draw children (of whatever chronological age) to theatre but to convince adults (of whatever chronological age) to return to it. The only imaginable product of the art of theatre is neither laughter nor applause, but silence in the face of the unspeakable horrors and joys it presents as a basis for new imaginings. Silence is borne best not by the young, but by those who recognize it as a prospectus of the future. It is beyond hope and hopelessness, optimism and pessimism. It does not teach, nor congratulate, nor flatter itself for its easy empathy and right-thinking, nor is it either true or false. You can neither agree nor disagree with it; it is there, beyond the easy confines of one's agreement with it. It is an art of theatre that barely exists. But it is the only theatre I feel it necessary to create, and just about the only theatre I care to witness.

§ 59

Joy. There are some who would consider the provision of joy to be the mission of theatre or art, to its audience or to its practitioners. Most also believe that government should subsidize this provision, perhaps even as a "public good." (Their propagandist slips are showing; the provision of sorrow, pain or tragedy, of the mirror of a fragmented experience, certainly of the individual imagination over the collective celebration, is not a public good, but its opposite.) A thin line exists between provision of joy and its imposition upon the audience or the culture, which laps it up as readily as it would any self-congratulatory treat. As an aesthetic end, the provision of joy is the provision of a cold, lifeless, collective thing, a dead-end street: a blinder to darker experience. Attempting to convince itself of its validity in the face of this experience, collective joy is a weapon to silence, marginalize and destroy the darker imagination. The tragic suggests that there is more, a path to freedom that may contain a joy and ecstasy to be drawn from the path, but much else besides, but as this dilutes or undermines the simple pleasure it is best ignored and passed over in silence. The joy infantilizes, without pain and a rigorous determination and discipline of self-determination and self-fashioning, it is simple and childish. It is a joy that leads to the continuation and valorization of ignorance rather than knowledge. The blinder is tightened ...

§ 60

Skin, veil. The flesh is a tender fabric, as language is a tender noise. The costume is draped over the body is as music draped over sound, words draped over thought, expression: there's your elegance. The turn of the leg (caught but sensed beneath the lithe and cool fabric), the breath of the player, the word's syllable suggest the passion, pleasure, ecstasy beneath. They simultaneously restrain and express the unfathomable possibilities for suffering and pleasure within—necessary disciplined restraint, necessary expression, for public exhibition. (Street clothes, which turn the body ugly and sexless, have no place in the theatre. Uncomfortable? Transgression and anxiety, desire, are uncomfortable—they lead to trembling, not relaxation.) Is it any wonder that we insist on couture and lyricism in the art and especially the silence of our theatre? The consciousness of the audience reflects the metaphors of costume and sound, its reflection thrown back upon itself (unbridgeable distance between spectator and performer, even as they so painfully seek to join), but transfigured in lace, silk, animal skin, sentences. Drama is the scalpel that cuts through costume, thought, sound so tenderly, piercing the veil of the phenomenon ...

§ 61

Maskwork. Faces becoming the reflections of screens: Digital and neon light reflected off the flesh, drawing off the blood. Following on the masks of Greek theatre, the contemporary theatrical face itself reflects another manufactured persona already, imposed by video, film, the Internet. A form of cold death, imitation of imitation and Baudrillard's hyperreality. Theatre now rejects the mask; the human face itself reflecting the sun's light or the dark of the night is a mask sufficient.

§ 62

The face in the theatre. The Athenian Theatre of Dionysus held approximately 12,000 people, necessitating the use of masks that exaggerated the facial features of the performers behind them. Although very few theatre workers today have such large auditoria at their disposal, the distance between spectator and performer remains great enough that performers continue to exaggerate their expressions (hence "mugging," the root word of which is a slang synonym for "face"). Because the spectator has his full attention on the stage in front of him, these expressions are experientially magnified. Thoughtful directors realize this even today, that the smallest change in facial expression can communicate considerable information.

The human face is a unique performative instrument. Not only does it contain all of the sense organs (eyes, ears, nose, mouth, skin) through which the representations of the world outside of us are created, it is also the unique object of subjectivity:

that immediate object which maintains a delicate balance between subjective expression (through the mouth that speaks, the musculature of the face) and empirical perception. The face expresses and receives impressions. In such guise it is a fetish for the personality within, behind it: another mask behind which is the protean, undefinable self.

Though most auditoria are too large to fully exploit the face's possibilities, in small theatres, where exaggeration is neither necessary nor welcome, the performer's face is a uniquely expressive instrument. Although the body moves as well, it is the face that can contain the dramatic event, moment to moment. It is surprising that more directors don't recognize this possibility of the human face, especially in smaller theatres, where both physical and facial gestures tend to be far too large for the room: grimaces and grins, rather than moments of tender intimacy between performer and spectator.

In a chamber theatre, the face takes center stage, its features of particular power, even more so than the human body; if the body is immediate object, the face is the conduit between the subjective and objective, the noumenal and phenomenal worlds. "Perhaps the fact that [my lips] move is more significant ... than the words which come through them," said Ruth in *The Homecoming*. The chamber theatre allows us to "read" these lips, not only for the words that come through them, but for those as well in the language of lyrical and dramatic tragedy.

And, in such a small confined space as a 50-seat theatre, to offer the face itself as sacrifice to the audience. In his discussion of the surfaces of the body, especially the face, Alphonso Lingis in *The Community of Those Who Have Nothing in Common* describes what is offered by performer and spectator in the metaphorical arena of the theatre space itself, for the face is within that metaphorical reach, can more easily cross that distance between stage and audience, the eye taking the place of the hand. I hope it is also clear that the performer caresses with her words, her movements, her face as well, and that in this tension between performer and spectator lies the possibility for tragic recognition:

> The surfaces of the other, as surfaces of susceptibility and suffering, are felt in the caressing movement that troubles my exploring, manipulating, and expressive hand. For the hand that caresses is not investigating, does not gather information, is not a sense organ. It extends over a surface where the informative forms soften and sink away as it advances, where agitations of alien pleasure and pain surface to meet it and move it. The hand that caresses does not apprehend or manipulate; it is not an instrument. It extends over a surface which blocks the way to the substance while giving way everywhere; it extends over limbs which have abandoned their utility and intentions. The hand that caresses does not communicate a message. It advances repetitively, aimlessly, and indefatigably, not knowing what it wants to say, where it is going, or why it has come here. In its aimlessness it is passive, in its agitation it no longer moves itself; it is moved by the passivity, the suffering, the torments of pleasure and pain, of the other.
>
> What recognizes the suffering of the other is a sensitivity in my hands, in my voice, and in my eyes, which finds itself no longer moved by my own imperative but by the movements of abandon and vulnerability of the other. This sensitivity extends not to order the course and heal the substance of the other, but to feel the feeling of the other. The movement of this sensitivity recognizes the surfaces of the other as a face appealing to me and putting demands on me. It recognizes the imperative that com-

> mands the other ordering me also. What recognizes the suffering of the other is a movement in one's hand that turns one's dexterity into tact and tenderness; a movement in one's eyes that makes it lose sight of its objectives and turn down in a recoil of respect; and a movement in one's voice that interrupts its coherence and its force, confuses its concepts and its reasons, and troubles it with murmurs and silence.[41]

§ 63

Body of words, body of text. The dramatist writes with regard to his words as fleshed in space, not inked on paper, which opens the play of physical signifiers and signifieds in language and in the performing body. He speaks tyrant and victim, beggar and emperor, woman and man, which he finds within himself. He unleashes the possibilities of flesh and its representations, all of its organs and sensations free for the exchange with those of an auditor in the dark. Flesh, blood, hand, eye, phallus, womb: the physical evidences of gender and engendering themselves freed for imagination. They are traded and exchanged through the writing body, the speaking body, the hearing and watching body, representations caught, caressed and tossed back again. Symbology made flesh. Words that penetrate, and welcome penetration, and exchange visions, world constructs, perceiving selves and ecstasy. (This is far beyond youth, chronological and psychological, especially beyond the blind adolescent self-love of most contemporary theatre and those who populate its arenas: sexualities become more textured with age, as the body matures and changes, possibility broadens, closer towards the end of its days.)

---

41 Alphonso Lingis, *The Community of Those Who Have Nothing in Common*. Bloomington, IN: Indiana University Press, 1994, pp. 31-32.

Closing distances, to inhere in a new self, composed of dramatist, performer, auditor together. New bodies born ...

The highest artifice, the disciplined theatre. Torturous distance separating physical selves. But not for that reason any the less *real*, indeed far from *surreal* (especially the closed surreality of the deadly, final interpretation of a dream, which the art of theatre most assuredly rejects), perhaps more real for their attempted expression ...

§ 64

Primer. All live performance is a passing away of time and the body: this dying is the primer, the medium, upon which all theatrical and performative activity is imposed; in its wake nothing, mere memory that fades and dies away as well. It is at the heart of all live performance; in common with the performer the audience is passing away also, decaying, bodies experiencing the curse of time together. But then: what does one say, what does one imagine, what does one see (anew), what sounds does one make and can be heard, what stain upon the silence, what other kind of life emerges. Something towards ecstasy, in common, and recognition, in common, and a new way of looking at the world in common, new avenues of imagination, perception and possibility. A drama that attracts those who share these elective affinities. Theatre's only conceivable *relevance* and *vitality* lie in this acceptance and revelation ...

§ 65

The authoritarian anecdote. I don't trust the anecdote. The anecdote presumes the validity of the consciousness from which it emerges—the anecdote is valid, on this score, only to the extent of the trustworthiness of the person telling it. But he always has his own agenda to pursue. It is true *only insofar as it convinces the listener*, who may or may not be willing to enter into that consciousness; if the ground of its telling is open to question, or subverted, suddenly the anecdote's power dissipates. It is a confidence game; the anecdotalist attempts to win my confidence; he tries to take me within his own; and if he does, I lose, sap that I've proven myself to be.

Most dramatic plots are collections of anecdotes: first this happens, then this, then this (each "this" an anecdote, chained together into what the undergraduate playwriting textbooks call a "narrative arc"). What interests me are the interstices between the anecdotes, how one leads to the other; though I like a good anecdote myself, there's more to theatre than that. (Bars are very good places for anecdotes, but I go to the theatre for other reasons.) It is only in these interstices that my imagination has play, that the play allows me, as an audience member, to become creative myself. The anecdotist who doesn't allow me to imagine, who directs me down one specific narrative avenue without deviation, filling in those spaces, becomes a tyrant over my imagination. In his easy intimacy, in his personableness itself, he draws me in to subsume me.

The erotic aphorist, on the other hand, confronts me with the contradictions inherent within my preconceptions in an attempt to overturn them, to find a new conceptual possibility. Confidence is not even an issue; confidence is irrelevant. The surprise of aphorism is in its contradiction of established wisdom, including my own. An aphorism proves itself, it doesn't prove the validity of a worldview. In confronting and challenging me so, the theatre artist frees my eyes to wander over his play: they can roam at liberty, having had the ground shaken (and respectfully so) beneath them, and perhaps find a new unexpected object or person on his stage to caress ... So my attention wanders, freely and most creatively, in his theatre. I am not rapt by his creation; I create myself, in all senses of those words, in both the transitive and intransitive forms of the verb. And I am not trapped by the anecdotist's need to be respected and well-liked. Nobody should be an artist just to make new friends.

The theatre artist might give others the courage to become erotic aphorists themselves, in their own lives, and give themselves up to the possibilities for renewed life within their reawakened imaginations.

§ 66

Two forms of spectacle. The first: that which is revelatory when the dramatist writes his self, the performer gestures hers, creating and unveiling body and spirit in word, speech and movement. In the study and the rehearsal room (the sites of discipline) following exploration, the dramatist un-writes that which is not the self and its world, chipping away the detritus of the quotidian; the performer pulls back, un-performs the inessential. The work is in the unveiling of the self, the tearing apart of the veil, the fabric of the curtain woven from trivia. (The fabric of a sensuous costume reveals the body beneath it. In the moment of sexual ecstasy, and of suffering, nothing but the essentials of sound and body adhere to the self, are communicated one to the other.) No wonder that the work needs to be careful, its teasing time-consuming, long and difficult, pursued without compromise.

The second: that which hides, which draws new curtains over the self and the world. Curtains of flashing light and loud noise, concealing torture and lusts for power even as it welcomes laughter and cheap wonder. A blanket that drowns the self and world. A light that blinds, a noise that deafens, the self. This is the condition of the contemporary drama. A spectacle that *hides*, rather than *reveals*, and rewards only our infantile or animal attraction to sound and light. In its pretense to human warmth, it commodifies emotion, our sense of wonder, manipulates it, cold and sterile: no life comes from it. It lies. Entertainment for dull children who desire deception and distraction, who fear the mature body's possibilities and inevitable tragedy ...

Of the second spectacle we have the contemporary manifestations of industrialized television, film, sport, politics. All well suited to the second. Is that not enough, or must the art of theatre operate under its subsumation as well, instead of in conflict with it? As if the screens, from those above Times Square to those we carry in our pockets, were not numerous enough. If the theatre is uniquely suited for the first kind of spectacle, its most significant arena, why pursue or praise the second? The suspicion that there is not enough *time* in these years of ours (of mine) for both. ...

§ 67

Nightlanguage; nightwork. A common trope of near-death experiences is the invitation of the dying by the dead, by heaven, into the light—a not inappropriate trope for the contemporary American theatre, which similarly draws its audience into a death of imagination through the light of its entertainment.

As the illumination of the electric light has more and more thrust theatre into its status as a primarily nighttime art (both the Greeks and Shakespeare wrote their plays for a daytime theatre structure), the contemporary theatre, through its fear of the dark and the night, has become brighter, despite the fact that the art of theatre is now properly an art of the dark, its proper language a Joycean "nightlanguage." David Ian Rabey in a 2006 interview with Daniel Meyer-Dinkgrafe draws dramatic language and dramatic work together:

> ... I favor drama which works in terms of what Brendan Kennelly terms nightenglish which reaches beyond reason in its surprising and speculative interrogative presences, rather than the day-english of rational communication and explanation which is usually predicated on some utilitarian terms, beyond those of the theatre itself. ...
>
> The demands of what might, appropriately in this context, be termed my "day job" inevitably tend to take precedence: the busyness of exposition and explanation in teaching students, the placating of bureaucratic demands which are ... all I suppose in the service of the (sometimes heartwarmingly) ludicrous attempt to make a living and raise a family. *But then there is the nightwork, in individual imaginings or interpersonal encounters and rehearsal, which yields its own promptings, and becomes resentful if denied for too long. ...*[42] [Emphasis added.]

What the dark of the night (and the dark of the theatre) requests is an experience beyond the merely visual, the object distanced from us but recognisable; in the dark, in the night, denied our daytime eyes, the touch of our flesh is hyper-sensitised; what is it that we are feeling, what impinges upon our bodies unrecognizable and unseen? A language and perspective which under-

---

42 Daniel Meyer-Dinkgrafe, *Views, Positions, Legacies: Interviews with German and British Theatre Artists, 1985-2007*. Newcastle: Cambridge Scholars' Publishing, 2007, p. 137.

scores that fleshed status: that provokes our imagination to unexpected because unseen sites of experience.

The light of entertainment is perverse because it means the death of the individual imagination and possibility; it may be that we are so passionately in love with the flickering pixel, with the light that pretends to show us truth (a corporately-constructed truth out of the culture factories of mass media and capitalism), that we can no longer feel a touch on our own flesh. The entirely visual field of the hysterically kinetic and hyperdestructive videogame and film, subsumed in lighted death.

The trope is corrupted but ecstatically so. Now, night and darkness are life and possibility: the theatre as a nighttime art is in its proper place. The speaking flesh in the dark seduces. We can't see its source; is it speaking to us? Is that the speaker's cool hand we feel on our forearm? Of course death and pessimism still play around the dark night, as they must, and it is the dark perhaps that we daytime beings fear the most. We are most at risk there. And there is something to this, that the dark night too is the refuge of death as well as life. But we must resist the urge to moralize and cut off the possibility of a more ecstatic existence.

Can a word emerging from the dark seduce and excite us, even when the speaking body is distant? Most emphatically, yes, though no one can answer in the positive without having experienced that himself. In this recognition we realize the power of language, for ourselves and in others.

Instead of inviting the audience into the light of the stage, the art of theatre invites them into the nightworld surrounding it, defining that nightworld with its negative illuminatory space.

It is this sublime ecstasy that Schopenhauer experiences in aesthetic, musical and theatrical epiphany, an epiphany verging on the mystical. It is a nighttime ecstasy, fully charged with the unconscious will, and containing within it the deepest wounds and most ecstatic caresses of the fleshed word. This is, perhaps, what those who condemn these so-called philosophical pessimists refuse to see, whether it's from sloppy reading, or from only a glancing familiarity with the primary text itself, or from judging these "pessimists" (including Beckett and Bernhard) having read only a paragraph in the secondary literature here or a book jacket there. They misread deliberately, or dismiss superficially, for many of these are cold and impatient wonders. They fear the possibilities of the life of the night. Whereas even Schopenhauer, giving life, fathered a daughter ...

§ 68

Homo sum: humani nil a me alienum puto. The ameliorist theatre, a fully-paid subsidiary of the culture industry, would prefer to think otherwise: that so many things human are alien to its audiences, that so many human possibilities for the experience of suffering and ecstasy are beyond their capabilities. An insult to imagination of both audience and practitioner. "Evil" (a useless distinction that distances the possibilities for our own behavior into something outside of us, some amorphous abstract cloud) is particularly, it says, beyond us as a collective and as individuals (though "good" is always so conveniently inherent in us as a collective and as individuals, we needn't worry about that). Heinous acts are always committed by others, never ourselves: the deepest pain and abuse, the highest ecstasy and pleasure are then excepted from our art. Because human they inevitably arise in the artistic creation, but in a culture of laughter (and comedy, in its effort to undermine all sublime experience with a joke that releases rather than retains tension, is the truly cathartic form, *contra* Aristotle) these experiences serve as fodder for amusement. Instead of being a way into a deeper recognition, a joke is utilized as a means of deflecting, defanging that recognition. Betrayal, abuse, corruption, compromise, abjectness, ecstasy, pleasure—all human individuals are capable of all these, all have a place in the theatre, but the ameliorist theatre denies them, rendering them a part of the non-human. In a politically progressive age dedicated to the ideals of a corrupted enlightenment, the theatre is blind. It remembers the humanist ideals of the beginning of the French and Russian Revolutions and pretends to forget the rapid descent of both movements into grotesque barbarism, though it's the high ideals that are abstract, the bloodied barbarism that is bodied (cf. Büchner's *Danton's Death*). The ameliorist theatre, the culture industry, dreams pretty dreams of the human experience, condemns the spectrum of human experience to a pallid monotonous mediocrity. The art of theatre awakens its practitioners and audiences to the very real darkness—as well as the possibility for imaginative and ecstatic freedom—that surrounds it.

Though a play must not be moralistic and therefore a sermon, it always is a moral act. The condition of a pallid and puritanical culture's theatre is thus a reflection of its pallid and puritanical morality and ethics.

§ 69

All abstract time, past and future, is contained in the present moment, the only time that is not an abstraction, as even animals know: the moment of our birth (and that of the world), the moment of our death (and that of the world) both inhere in the present breath. The theatrical performance is a succession of present moments: necessarily a process of erasure of the past and extension into the future. Comedy looks back to the first terminus, its memory ever-present, tragedy forward to the second, its fact inescapable. Only silence touches on what lies before and after us in the world; noise and laughter distract us from it. In terms of form, duration stretches the present moment and holds it open for examination. Comedy as a genre seeks to cut it short as soon as possible, hence its speed (and its noise and its desperate need to amuse and comfort). Tragedy steeps us in the present, and that knowledge of the moment of our death, which exists in this time, in this theatre. It provides no escape. This is the basis of Proust's own conception of time, deadening habit preventing us from living in full knowledge and potential of the present moment. To habit and the illusion of well-being, the full realization of the present moment's potential is catastrophic. This is the specific power of Sophoclean tragedy. And therefore *Krapp's Last Tape*, *Old Times*, *No Man's Land*, and longer works from Morton Feldman, in which time is the subject. Like the present body, the presence of death in the theatre is inescapable, and its end.

Only that person who lives in full knowledge and acceptance of that death lives fully, accepts its sublimity, and touches on what lies beyond it. T.S. Eliot, in "Burnt Norton":

> Words move, music moves
> Only in time; but that which is only living
> Can only die. Words, after speech, reach
> Into the silence. Only by the form, the pattern,
>
> Can words or music reach
> The stillness, as a Chinese jar still

Moves perpetually in its stillness.
Not the stillness of the violin, while the note lasts,
Not that only, but the co-existence,
Or say that the end precedes the beginning,
And the beginning and the end were always there
Before the beginning and after the end.
And all is always now.

§ 70

"Art is the lie that tells the truth." Much as many would like to place emphasis on the last word of that statement, the simple, unadorned, unqualified direct object of the sentence is "lie"—that is, artifice, as in "art." Whatever truth value may inhere in the experience of theatre, it inheres *ex post facto* and not within the experience itself. Similarly, there is no "magic" in theatre; if we are to insist on precision, we must insist on art's status as illusionism, as something of this world and not beyond it. In citing the experience of art as supernatural, we deny responsibility for it, and our reaction to it. Theatre is discipline, nothing is accomplished there through the mere wave of a wand. We react through our bodies, in which our souls inhere.

The idea that art is magic or truth is more destructive in the realm of explicitly political theatre, for explicitly political theatre, more than any other, insists on its own validity, its own truth-value. You will not hear from the self-righteous practitioners of this theatre the statement, "We are telling lies"; this would, more than anything else, undermine if not completely invalidate its own status. Hence the inevitable inefficacy of theatre that aims to be politically, socially or culturally relevant. The lies that art tells have value, but their value is not in political, ameliorist or utilitarian truth. Neither will wars, nor suffering, nor tragedy end with the mere wave of a wand.

The art of theatre is a cold hard thing at its heart. It is a knife-edge, not a feather or a salve.

§ 71

The play as erotic aphorism. There is an intense need in the decision to work aphoristically: that there is so much to say, so little time to say it in, with too few resources. The most economically and environmentally sound of method, aphorism squeezes each last theatrical, aural and literary drop from each and every movement, sound and word. (So it is the most lyrical, too, of forms.) The fragility of time is such that with each second we can slip from it; millions in the past century have learned that time can be torn asunder with a knock at the door or a flash in the sky (millions more in the last, most technological, democratic, humanistic and enlightened century than in any century before, a fact which interests no-one, certainly not in the theatre). Those who create dramatic aphorisms tie crisp, brisk Gordian knots of theatre. The well-turned, tight-bodied word explores a possibility of unexpected ecstasy in the surprise of its making, in the connection of flesh and sound. Destroy this with analysis or with meaning-making, and you can't put it back together again.

As with Webern and Celan, each sound, each word expands in all dimensions of space and time simultaneously. Even the interstitial silences and stillnesses bear weight. Calling attention to themselves (not out of the self-love of the Broadway musical and the downtown epic alike, but rather because there is nothing else to hear or see), they demand tender attention and compassion for the painful rips they inflict upon the darkness.

Environmentally, too: ambitious design sprawls like a soft, manicured and unnecessary suburb around a hard city of experience. And ambitious longer forms rob the audience of time better spent with their lives than with our art. That we take their money in the name of entertainment is indicative of our absorption in the culture industry. "Of course, it's very funny, too": these words the self-serving rationale of a dead spirit, for we drown in comedy from every screen and page. There is no shortage of it. If we demand it even from our most sublime ambitions—ambitions beyond the lachrymose or the insipid—we reveal that we have been absorbed into that industry to the point of disappearance. We are no longer here, but within the hysterical screen.

In building a theatre that is necessary (necessary because like all necessary things it is imaginable and does not yet exist), I don't need a space of more than 50 seats, nor more than a few performers, nor the run of more than a half-dozen performances, nor more than an hour of an individual's time; a call even for this is self-aggrandizing. But one must offer something hard, and tight, and uncompromising, word, performance, self and body inextricably bound, like the most effective aphorisms, in the exchange.

§ 72

The object who knows. The performer is a privileged object on the stage: she is the Object Who Knows, the displayed perspective of tragedy. She is the figure in the physical landscape who sees it from inside, something quite beyond the poet, and in that sense lives within his construct. But because she lives within it, she is, unlike him, surrounded by it, must make her way. The performer who is brave, tenacious, is willingly absorbed by her surroundings, but in that absorption her power is her own consciousness. So she has power over performance, she shapes the air as much as the other objects and performers on the stage. The poet gives her words with which to valorize her consciousness of her condition.

The profoundly political stance of this condition, indeed the politically revolutionary status of erotic tragedy, inheres in the willing valorization of this consciousness. Performance is an ecstatic falling, all senses open and willing to experience what terrors and joys lie in wait for the tragic consciousness. As privileged Object Who Knows, she demonstrates her courage, her intent to transform the performance space into an arena of sensuous awareness. The audience may transform their world outside the theatre, armed with her example.

It is amoral work. The seeming frenetic nihilism however is captured and contained within the discipline of training, of the knowledge of how to see, to move, to appear. The performer's body is a landscape within a landscape, explored for her from within, the audience tracing the inner journey through her flesh. She possesses the power of her body to explore conventional morality, to explore transgression, as an individual agent. The meaning is the exploration; in exploration itself is political meaning, experiential possibility, the truly radical political stance. In that sense, the following is far more radically political than much American theatre that posits itself as such.

§ 73

"*The metaphor of childbirth which never seems to die.*" A poem, a play, is the chronicle of a perception: not the perception itself (which may be trite or complex, commonplace or rare, self-serving or altruistic), but a chronology of its emergence. This is how it exists in time, from beginning to end, and like birth, it is experience, not product. The poem describes it, its contours, as means of communicating its content.

The poem is procedure. The greatest task of the poet is discipline and care, not to write (or, at least, not merely write, and in this golden age of literacy everyone can), but to time, precision and specificity: to try to get it right the first time. Like an obstetrics manual, the poem must describe accurately, carefully, without baroque augmentation or unnecessary linguistic spectacle, the means to the expression of that unique perception. (In the realm of poetry and drama, spelling counts; one can't abuse or disregard the tools of expression without exposing our ignorance of their power, our lack of respect for written communication itself and those whom we're addressing, and the possibilities of experience words invite.) An obstetrics manual which indulges in platitude or moralism is quite as useless as a poem which does the same. At worst, inaccuracy and slop in the description can lead to death, of the child and its mother, or of the perception.

In any case, description can only follow experience; no amount of imagination, of frill, will be worthwhile if it is not grounded in direct perception. A poet might describe his own birth, but only if he has courageously sought it, and then that perception remains his own perception. He can only tell how he got there. The pain and the wound, too, remain his own. He cannot share, he cannot express, the self. "Self-expression" is not only meaningless, but, in the realm of art, impossible. Self is expressed in life, not in art. He can only instruct in the means of finding and exploring one's own.

§ 74

What she knew. To "write what you know," for a dramatist or for that matter for any other creative artist, is an easy trope to disseminate in the classroom or textbooks about writing. Creation is a form of knowing, of coming-to-know something that was previously unknown. If for the sake of argument we can even say that the word "knowledge" is appropriate, it is knowledge that comes through the process of creative discovery, of an imaginative entering into a landscape of the mind. Beauty is not an issue here; landscapes are not beautiful in and of themselves, they are cold hard things. Only the perspective of the observer can wrench a recognizable beauty from them. Knowledge is an examination of, a familiarity with, landmarks in that landscape. (And certainly discoverable, too, in music, as discoverable as these landmarks are when they're described with the spoken word.)

In that destructive trope is supposedly a recipe for creation: the easy definition, in that what is known is history, memory, science, experience. But that is not knowledge of a landscape; that is trivia, grist for the imagination. Bodies in that landscape, too, can be entered, discovered; the explorer finds recognizable features of the lay of his own land in the landscapes of others.

But it is possible to know. The title of my play about Jocasta is *What She Knew*, and it is only possible to explore that by entering her experience as the Sophoclean landscape presents it to me. Whether or not Jocasta is a fictitious character is immaterial; I can enter her body, her features, see a landscape through her eyes. And make notes, for the store of knowledge that I can then call upon when writing the words I would speak. But this is not study; it is experiencing imaginatively her body and landscape.

Because desire is recognizable, a common human trait, I already have this path into her.

But it is an imaginative path, education a dynamic process between perceiver and perceived. And it is amoral: Brecht's Galileo says "I must know," and it is the passion for knowing that leads him to defy the culture and the church. To find and express a new knowledge. Bearing Galileo in mind, it must be said that knowledge is not something one learns, one picks up in books, one sees through a telescope, or even within everyday experience or memory. It requires discipline and sacrifice. Knowledge is not to study, to remember, to learn. To know, the poet must dare.

§ 75

At first glance, the plays of Howard Barker and Samuel Beckett have precious little in common. Barker's anti-Histories, recent concern with plethora and excess and the aristocratic lyricism found in the dialogue of his characters sit uneasily with Beckett's abstract minimalism and self-erasing language. But a few minutes' thought reveals surprising parallels, especially when it comes to the later work of both dramatists. The spare theatrics and four-woman cast of Barker's *Slowly*, produced in 2010, reveal at least scenographic common traits with Beckett's three-woman *Come and Go*; *Hurts Given and Received*, also produced in 2010, is an essay on the cost of aesthetic creation also at the center of *Catastrophe*; and, reaching a little further back, the master/servant relationship of Toonelhuis and Lobe in 2009's *Found in the Ground*, as well as a decimated landscape, is surprisingly reminiscent of Hamm and Clov in Beckett's *Endgame* (even to the extent that both Toonelhuis and Hamm are confined entirely to wheelchairs; justice is also a theme in both plays as well). At least in these limited comparisons, there appears to be considerable aesthetic companionship, and no doubt another few minutes' thought would produce other parallels.

The later perspectives of both dramatists is also usefully considered through the prism of Arthur Schopenhauer's philosophy, in all four of its central facets (epistemology, metaphysics, aesthetics and ethics). For the theatreworker, even Schopenhauer's epistemology echoes through the basic construct of the aesthetic form of theatre. In the first book of *The World as Will and Representation*, as well as in Schopenhauer's doctoral thesis *On the Fourfold Root*, the philosopher lays out an epistemology that will not surprise either dramatist or director. The necessary forms of consciousness—those which exist *a priori* and without which knowledge and consciousness, and therefore the empirical world, are not possible—are there described as Time, Space and Causality, this last entry divisible into various forms (four altogether) of cause-and-effect. Turning to the first page of any conventional drama, one finds these *a priori* forms stated as givens of the drama to follow. Time (today, the next day, yesterday, the 16th century); place (a crossroads marked by a tree, a bunker, Vienna); and finally a list of characters, demonstrating the forms of human motival relationships possible within the confines of the play, the narrative for which itself is based in the cause-and-effect relationships of the physical world (in movement) and conceptual world (in language). Any and all theatre is constructed of these *a priori* forms, without which something presented on a stage can't be said to be theatre *qua* theatre, any more than, without these, the empirical world can't be represented as the empirical world.

Since the *ur*-Modernist Schopenhauer, whose most pessimistic assessments about the world and the will were more than borne out in the history of the twentieth century, Modernists have been investigating and stressing these *a priori* concepts in their own art as well, seeking through this stress an inference of the thing-in-itself that lies beneath the empirical world; theatre as the most phenomenal of these forms is where those stresses have been most tortuous. In the later plays of both Beckett and Barker, there has been less certainty about a definable time, space and causality as expressed in character and narrative, until in the work of both writers the only thing that can be said with any certainty is that this work is taking place here, in this space; now, at this time; and through the individuals we see on stage: the immediacy of the theatrical experience is nowhere more explicit than in the plays of these dramatists. The stress and intensity of the work, as well as its seeming difficulty and obtuseness, is an effect ultimately of both dramatists' projects to find through their work an inference of the thing-in-itself that lies beyond the empirical world: ultimately unknowable, but somehow demonstrable. It is reminiscent of Beckett's early statement to a correspondent that his work exists to "To bore one hole after another in [language], until what lurks behind it—be it something or nothing—begins to seep through; I cannot imagine a higher goal for a writer today."[43] While this may best describe Beckett's consideration of prose fiction at the time, it is just as applicable to his art of drama, once space, time, character and narrative are also seen as those empirical forms which must be compromised to reach a

---

43 Samuel Beckett, *Disjecta: Miscellaneous Writings and a Dramatic Fragment*. Edited by Ruby Cohn. New York: Grove Press, 1984, p. 171.

gleam of the thing-in-itself in a contemplative or meditative state.

Barker's language differs from Beckett's in that his characters pour out character and motivation, and the director and designers fill the stage with painterly and precise excess, expressively—so expressively that the language overwhelms, the power of aristocratic eloquence turns in upon itself and, like Beckett's minimal speech, bores similar holes through *a priori* experience, utterly destroying the "either/or" dichotomy that most contemporary drama and theatre offer, per David Ian Rabey, for a "both/and" status of the theatrical experience.[44]

The work of both dramatists also bears examination through the prisms of Schopenhauer's metaphysics, aesthetics and ethics: this last an ethics of compassion. Beckett asks for an understanding compassion for the fallen condition even of the Pozzos and Hamms of his world, a compassion which is their due, as is Katrin's, Galactia's and that of several other Barker characters, from those populating *The Castle* and *Victory* to *Gertrude—The Cry* and *Found in the Ground*. The road to this compassion is severe and calls into question the accepted forms of the empirical world to search further, for an aesthetic experience that will make compassion possible for the spectator. But this is to get to Schopenhauer's fourth book already, and there are further paths to be cleared before it emerges clearly. It is here that the parallels between these great dramatists, who may well emerge as the Shakespeares of the twentieth and twenty-first century, may

---

44 For an extended discussion of the "either/or" and "both/and" dichotomies, see the introduction of David Ian Rabey, *English Drama Since 1940*. Harlow: Longman, 2003, pp. 1-5.

demonstrate the possibility of a theatre in the wake of catastrophe.

§ 76

It may now be appropriate to begin the discussion of theatre as the ideal arena for the public expression and investigation of erotic love.

Following upon the melancholy metaphysics of Schopenhauer and Adorno's baleful portrait of the late twentieth century, this will require the utter destruction and closure of theatre and drama as it is practiced today and a reconstruction, from the ground up, of its possibilities for the expression of this erotic love, in which there may be the only true hope (if not possibility) for a redemption of the body and the spirit. As theatre in its commercial and non-commercial institutional forms has become marginalized in the cultural life of the community, drowned out by the far more accessible electronic and print mass media, it continues to serve a function as a pale shadow of its former status which partook, during its time, of an acknowledgement of this erotic love. Now, theatre envies the television, movie and computer screen their ubiquity, and wishes ridiculously to ape that ubiquity. It is impossible, and so it must go.

That said, the new theatre acknowledges itself as sexual fetish, as it operates from within a rigorous, disciplined structural form which substitutes object for other object, as each word, prop, costume and body on a stage points to another off that stage; the provision of eroticism to these words and costumes glow, however, with the possibility of their private enactment. At the same time it is not celebration, for it must needs express the tragic impossibility of the final liberation from suffering that temporary non-existence in the moment of joined orgasm suggests. This requires an extraordinary imagination for the self, the writer, the performer and the spectator, to draw into the theatre space all taboo and, more, to take these taboos as serious though abject expressions of the human spirit. There is Eros even in paralysis, in restraint as well as limbed freedom, as the spirit reaches for that Nirvana-like non-existence with another.

The contemporary theatre is ill-prepared for such an investigation and it cannot occur within the current progressive ideological construct which it shares with the culture that surrounds it, whether that culture is the marketplace, the academy, the town hall or the local community center. Not least because these cultures and ideologies perceive the sensual, the erotic, as avenues towards the same progressive utilitarianism as the government office or the television show: for titillation at worst, for self-aggrandizement and self-congratulation at best. Sexuality is not that; "sexuality is literally a killer," Howard Barker said, and what it kills is certainty.

In the introduction to his 1997 book *Foreign Bodies*, Alphonso Lingis locates the point of frisson between Eros and the administered culture, also implying the role that Agamben's concept of "biolife" plays in the dynamic of these two opposed metaphysics—a dynamic best demonstrated by the work of Shakespeare, Büchner, Barker, Rudkin and other dramatists of abjection:

> Foucault shows that the pleasure that simmers in our bodies is also coded, inciting the discourse and power operations of others. The power operations on our bodies as sensual substances do not simply oppress and suppress them; they diversify, differentiate, and incite, they produce a multiplicity of bodies individuated sexually. They subject them to the new biopolitical strate-

> gies of the modern state, strategies contrived for the administration and management of life.[45]

Lingis' work builds upon that of Georges Bataille, Jean-Luc Nancy and others who begin to be intent on the power of desire and Eros to reconfigure concepts of community, not the least of which the community that the theatrical and dramatic project represents, and where it is perhaps best explored: not to drag secrets into the light, but to explore the darkness with bodies and words, and feel the brush of flesh against flesh, unknown quantities and qualities, and the revelation of unexpected possibility. This is something the administered, transparent post-capitalist culture cannot admit, and so a space must be cleared for it in the theatre.

§ 77

Squaring the dark-suited, professorial librarian of Paris Georges Bataille with the first-person narrator of *Story of the Eye* or, for that matter, the philosopher of *Erotism* or *The Accursed Share* is an instructive affair. The wild imaginings of these writers are hard to find in the demeanor of the writers themselves. It points to a paradox of ecstasy and reserve in the most radicalized of writers. If one aspires to explore the farther reaches of imagination, it seems to suggest, one is well-advised to keep one's nose clean: to avoid offense in appearance or manner, in order to clear the way for the private imaginings conducted behind closed doors. But this is not all, for in the world of the casual week, never mind the casual Friday, this care in appearance and behavior, this leaning towards formality even in friendships, seems almost ostenta-

---

45 Alphonso Lingis, *Foreign Bodies*. New York: Routledge, 1994, p. x.

tious. And so it is. However, there is ostentation too in the self-conscious self-presentation of the apparent democratic populist, the friend of the working man and the oppressed: one sees it in Brecht especially, though Brecht, at least, retained that cultural radicalism and ambivalence. Inevitably, this behavior and costume betray a philistinism of which its subjects are proud: it is moral and aesthetic authoritarianism clad in a t-shirt, but authoritarianism nonetheless, partaking gladly of the offerings of the Culture Industry (whose products include styles of fashion and demeanor), subsuming a blind self in mad consumption. And thirsting for the power, influence and money to messianically change the world, always in his own image, and kill the autonomous individual human being through ignorance and distance. This is, today, the status quo, especially of theatre.

The pursuit of tragic experience, which takes us to the outer reaches of imagination, paradoxically flourishes in this formal milieu, which in the twenty-first century is subversive all on its own. The ladies and gentlemen of tragedy, then: even as their behavior, manner and mien seem to partake of high-bourgeois culture, it is a high-bourgeois culture of almost a hundred years ago and radical in our time. It denies the desire for power and influence, seeing through its transparency and smilingly shrugging at its vanity. (Money it wants too—so do we all—but earned rather than as its due merely for existing.) It partakes of glamour and style, even in behavior: moderation and a good-natured personability, a tendency towards self-control and restraint (an absence from projects which create new forms of individualized white noise, like virtual social networking within arenas owned by corporations; besides, we need the time and silence for the work) rather than an excess of personality; we keep our counsel; an eye towards how we are seen. And not seen—we are gathered at cocktail parties on the side. We are comfortable even in our uncomfortable though carefully chosen clothes, our costumes which hint at the elegant bodies beneath; our recognition of each other makes us a community; our imaginations soar in the tragic theatres we make. An elite, if self-elected for all that: but there are enough of us.

§ 78

The earliest we have of the tragedies of Sophocles, *Antigone*, was written when he was about 55 years old—a play which seems to limn the idealism of youth was the product of a man at least twice the age of his protagonist. A quality of tragedy is that of a recognition of human time and mortality, and therefore something of age, if not chronological age, then certainly meditative age, an age which can decoct and encompass decades of experience within the 75 minutes of a single play. The Culture Industry's emphasis on youth and comedy necessarily denies this dimension of tragedy, an emphasis which quickly devolves into a neurotic, narcissistic celebration of the ego and an assumption of innocence, not so much afraid of death as refusing to be troubled by its presence all around us, and especially afraid of being, in that old high-school sense, unpopular (or, in the lovely parlance of Victorian and Edwardian England, unclubbable). It is perhaps likely that those who embrace the products of the Industry are no longer capable of recognizing tragedy, certainly no longer capable of valuing it as more of a necessity than comedy, which it most certainly is. (One need only consider the most common responses to the presentation of contemporary tragedy in New York: a superficial respect [or disrespect] for the ancients and for

Shakespeare; silence, dismissal or childish mockery for the rest.) Because of tragedy's peculiarly elitist dimension, its experience is open even to these. But it must be sought and will not be given freely; there must be that exchange of gifts inherent in theatrical production.

Anyone who has visited a geriatric psychiatry unit will recognize the remnants and rediscovery of childhood in some of its patients. An old man babbles baby babbles; a woman counts "1, 2, 3" as if to hold on to consciousness in its most abstract form. What is profound about this recidivism of childhood is that it is a childhood without a future: it is a childhood poised on the edge of nothingness, trapped in the decayed body near death. And it gives the lie to the politically and culturally progressive mindset, for the culture's individual subjects wind up here. As will all of them, eventually: and for those who deny the knowledge provided by tragedy, who avoid it and instead search for it in bastard forms like dark comedy or melodrama, without a recompense for the spirit.

§ 79

Maurice Benn's study of the work of Georg Büchner suggests that Büchner may have been familiar with Schopenhauer's philosophy (*The World as Will and Representation* having been published in 1818, twenty years before the composition of *Woyzeck* in 1837, while Schopenhauer was still alive). "The world is chaos. Nothingness its due messiah,"[46] goes a line in *Danton's Death*, a

46 Georg Büchner, *Complete Plays, Lenz, and Other Writings*. Translated by John Reddick. New York: Penguin Books, 1994, p. 69.

line which echoes Schopenhauer's metaphysics (as well as the final line of *The World as Will and Representation* itself).[47]

Büchner demonstrated "a pessimism deeper and darker than any to be found in the previous history of German thought with the possible exception of Schopenhauer," Benn notes,[48] but I wish to point out in connection with *Woyzeck* the play's structural relationship to time, space and causality—the three qualities which constitute the perception of the empirical world, according to the philosopher. The notorious structural difficulties of the play, unresolved by Büchner, stem from a deviation from the classical form which still inheres in *Danton's Death* and *Leonce and Lena*. This classical form bears resemblances to the idea of the well made tragedy as it came down from Aristotle in antiquity, but in *Woyzeck* the unities are entirely shattered: locations and times shift with an arbitrary rapidity. And not merely that: the great personages, kings and queens, of classical tragedy, even of Shakespearean tragedy, are absent from Büchner's collection of soldiers, bourgeois professionals and criminals.

Woyzeck, in which we find the first tentative steps towards the modern tragedy, suggests an attempt at the aesthetic project in Schopenhauer to deny the highly-structured empirical mirror of the well-told story or the well-made plot: an empiricism, according to Schopenhauer, which necessarily denies a recognition of the Will or thing-in-itself. By the first half of the nineteenth cen-

---

47 "... we freely acknowledge that what remains after the complete abolition of the will is, for all who are still full of the will, assuredly nothing. But also conversely, to those in whom the will has turned and denied itself, this very real world of ours with all its suns and galaxies is—nothing." Arthur Schopenhauer, *The World as Will and Representation: Volume I*. New York: Dover Publishing, 1966, pp. 411-412.

48 Maurice B. Benn, *The Drama of Revolt: A Critical Study of Georg Büchner*. Cambridge: Cambridge University Press, 1979, p. 61.

tury, the status of Reason as a controlling factor in the government of men had been seriously compromised by the bloody failures of the French Revolution to provide that democratic egalitarianism promised by the leaders of that revolution.

It may, perhaps, have been a reactionary turn of the theatre in the face of that failure towards the well-made domestic plays of the Victorian era: it was the era of Sardou and a little later Pinero, highly-constructed plots that were based most immovably in time, space and logical causality. It should also be noted that Schopenhauer preferred the tragedies of Shakespeare to those of the ancient Greeks, and one must note too that the stories of Shakespeare's plays are often extraordinarily ill-built from the point-of-view of logical development. *Hamlet* constructs a bewilderingly incomplete series of family, personal and political relationships, only to have nearly all of the characters die at the end from a combination of arbitrary chance, accident and spite. In nearly all the Shakespeare tragedies, everyone dies at the end: death as a *deus ex machina* to cut off, if not tie up, any loose ends of the plot. This is, from a classical view, poor storytelling. And additional proof, if any were needed, that it is not the story that drives the Shakespearean tragedy, but the language.

The desire of some contemporary theatre practitioners to put "a good story" on the stage (by which they seem to mean a narrative that follows a logical plot development and persuasive if commonplace psychological characterization) demonstrates a refusal to consider the drama as an avenue to exploring the catastrophic expression of the noumenal reality within the phenomenal world. Indeed, the phrase "getting lost in a story" is more than just a desire for a blinding enchantment: it is a fetishization of the phenomenal. This is of an entirely different nature than the contemplation of the noumenal that forms the center of Schopenhauer's aesthetic experience: for it is catastrophe that is contemplated, rather than an easy curiosity served. The contemporary well-made story brings blindness rather than knowledge.

§ 80

The degendering and regendering of Agamemnon in the final moments of the play that bears his name is central to the tragic consciousness. Clytemnestra strips her husband of his martial attire and catches him in "rich robes"—a feminization that he cannot escape, and a feminization that he welcomes at the hands of his wife. Similarly Oedipus' crime is haunted by both the death of his father and the erotic appeal of his sister/wife; the great quartet of Shakespearean tragedies too is centered in desire and gendered indefinition (Lear is not desexed, but his sexuality is mirrored in his female daughters, who themselves take on the mantle of masculinist power that Lear himself sloughs from his [S]overeign body). In Shakespeare the greatest nexus of Eros, the will and death occurs in *Antony and Cleopatra* and *Troilus and Cressida*, in which gender and desirous will circulate freely among the characters, offering ecstasies and terrors unbearable.

These ecstasies and terrors accompany knowledge of the Other, for Eros does circulate. It is a desirousness for identity with that phenomenal Other, his or her body, and through that identity a recognition and experience of the will in its most sublime manifestation, an avenue to the single thought that "The world is the self-knowledge of the will."

Even Schopenhauer did not recognize the most radical nature of sexual desire, this nature inhering in the metaphysics of tragedy. The theatre is unique in that the play of sexual signifiers among gesture, body and language can penetrate to aesthetic demonstration, once again a triangulation among first character, second character and spectator: and not the sexual act itself, but the circulation of Eros. In comedy, orgasm is the product; in tragedy, it is erotic imagination; in comedy, titillation; in tragedy, woundedness, tragic alienation from the world and Other, and ecstasy. Our currently non-tragic theatres are arenas for titillation and mutual masturbation, not the circulation of an erotic possibility that has profound phenomenal consequences in the relations among men, women and the world. The Culture Industry turns gender, sensuality and sexual preference into corporatized T-shirts: products to purchase; badges; marketing slogans.

Erotic possibility inheres in the circulation of these sexual signifiers as erotic transgressive poetry and the erotic transgressive body, married within the tragic aesthetic. They are shared between Agamemnon and Clytemnestra, Antony and Cleopatra, Tristan and Isolde (or, more recently, in the bodies of Jan Fabre's *Je Suis Sang* and Howard Barker's *The Twelfth Battle of Isonzo*). Among these characters the phallus and the womb—the erect cock, the damp cunt, the sexualized mouth and asshole—are shared, passed from character to character, given and possessed freely; in undermining cultural and social definition, the Procrustean beds of what it means to be either masculine or feminine, the spirit's redefinition of gender and ecstatic possibility are found. The will, the thing-in-itself, knows of no separation of masculine and feminine; it is the phenomenal world that does; in the agony of separation tragedy inheres. The cock, the cunt, brushes the soft and pregnant belly, the skin, externalized in fashion and costume, sung in the spoken word; tragedy bears the ecstatic sensation.

§ 81

I love ... Within tragedy this is the darkest, bloodiest truth, insofar as there is any truth value at all in tragedy. The phrase underlies all individual and family experience, guides the body and the words, impels the performer to make her offering and joins audience and dramatist in the descent into the dark abyss. Such words may be too powerful to be spoken in the Greek tragedies: in *King Lear,* its most searing metaphor is Cordelia's silence. Its most powerful expression then is metaphor detached from metaphor, a metaphor with all signifiers open to transformation and transgression: the possibility of tragedy is in the simultaneous egoism and surrender, the profound compulsive desire for union with the Other, the One. Transgressive metaphor fleshed and costumed. Tragedy succeeds when the profound human rhythm—the heartbeat, playing arhythmically and threaded through its regular beat with the shocks of experience and ecstasy—that this represents is felt in blood, in communal jointure. The phrase repels entertainment, simple pleasures and pains, in favor of the complex ecstasy and grueling terror it implies. Both the laugh and the cry, in midst of disorientation, discipline and fear, are recognition of the rhythm.

In finding the language for its expression, the dramatist embodies himself in his characters, female and male alike, in willed nightmare. This is his investigation and research, and why the dramatist must be primary: he stages in the theatrical space the contours of his own fear, terror, pleasure, as precisely as he can, even as he accepts its cultural meaninglessness. The creative act of the performer is in this fleshing of "I love"; it is rendered procreative, as a gift, to her audience.

Epilogue:
The Origins of Tragedy

A few years ago, in a hospice outside Philadelphia, I watched my father die. Although he had been suffering from emphysema for several decades, it was not this that finally led to his death. For months, he had not had the desire nor the appetite to eat, except for the occasional hard candy and, more importantly, his daily allotment of blackberry brandy. This, coupled with increasingly large doses of morphine, dulled the pain that had begun with the necrosis of his intestinal tract, which had recently begun to perish of disuse. His gastrointestinal system was the first to fail, the others followed in short stead. This man, who stood in his prime at six-feet tall, could not have weighed more than 80 pounds at his death. I sat at his bedside alone, though he'd been unconscious upon my arrival the day before (the doctors having admitted that he was no longer "really there"), and watched as the life of the body seeped out in a final few breaths.

It is hard to say whether this slow starvation was entirely voluntary; I doubt it was, but perhaps it was also in its way a slow unconscious suicide. A few months earlier, my pregnant wife and I had visited him when he was still something of his mordant, witty self, a baseball or football game, which he always enjoyed, on the television; we expressed our hope that he'd still be alive to celebrate the birth of his first grandchild, and I suppose he seconded that hope in a way; but he died a month before Goldie was born. The love he would have undoubtedly borne for his granddaughter would not have been unlike the love he undoubtedly bore for his children, his friends, even his ex-wife, but it was finally not enough, weakened body perhaps not possessing the desire to continue on.

Many years before, in the 1970s, he had divorced my mother and since then, I believe, he had foregone the pleasures of romantic and sexual love, not unlike Beckett's Krapp, and instead faced a series of darknesses, greatly alleviated by affection, pride in his children and certain other pleasures, but darkness was at the center of his days. The marriage had obviously not been a happy one, with the exception of the pleasure he took in my brother and myself; my mother suffered from alcoholism, clinical depression and other severe mental illnesses from about 1962 on, and she suffers so to this day. Even then he had difficulty finding the appetite to eat, to fuel the beast of his body. He found a great deal of succor in music, in art, and in history as well, though his professional education was in electrical engineering and his parents' background was stoutly working-class—his father was a self-employed electrician, his mother (who once tried to commit suicide) a cleaning woman at a local school, his step-brother mentally challenged ("retarded," the medical community at the time would have it) and in and out of institutions before an early death in his twenties. He also during the last ten years of his life enjoyed bringing his experience to the classroom, teaching at the undergraduate electrical engineering lab at the University of Pennsylvania and enjoying the company of teachers and students considerably younger than himself. In all this, he was a peaceful man, despising violence and conflict, even anger, as futile and invariably destructive and vicious qualities.

The tragic consciousness is borne in experience, and this is merely a small part of my own. It should be said too that the origin of my own tragic consciousness is here, in my experience. True, it is fed by the great tragic thinkers and writers of the centuries, but they merely confirm and further inform my personal experience, and do not dictate it. All true philosophy, Schopenhauer noted, is rooted in the personal, as it must be.

The same is true of the tragic aesthetic. In a sense, I value and hope to create the art which would lend my father (and others like him, for being human he was not alone) comfort in his darkness, to somehow render the contemplation of it a valuable rather than a valueless knowledge. I do not fool myself that this has any particular meaning for politics or appeals to those who seek self-satisfaction and self-aggrandizement through their work or merely desire to entertain and be entertained. My father was also a participant in culture, in society, as aware in his own way, I think, of the torsions of culture and its effect on him as Schopenhauer's or Adorno's awareness was meaningful to themselves, even if he may have found these philosophers beyond his ken (though Beckett and O'Neill, I know from personal experience, were both great pleasures to him).

Simplistic and pious hope to him was puerile; his experience taught him that it was foolish. Love and desire, he also knew, were fraught with both ecstasy and the greatest suffering. He was a deeply cynical and pessimistic man, but this cynicism and pessimism were based in his own life. He held no hope for progressive politics, the revelations of Hiroshima and Auschwitz fresh in his mind—John Hersey's book on the former had a prominent place on his bookshelf; these two events are still within living memory, if not for much longer, but for Americans all history is ancient, and increasingly irrelevant, history—despite having voted for Progressive Party candidate Henry Wallace in 1948, for Adlai Stevenson in 1952 and 1956, and finally John F. Kennedy in 1960, after which he did not participate in elections. His only hope lay in his children, I believe, of whom he was quite proud.

Not a day goes by since his death that I do not think of him in that last room, on that last bed, but not only there; I also think of him as time extends into the past from that last room, to his experience which is so much a part of my own. With the exploration of my own tragic consciousness, informed by experience, I hope to do some honor to his memory, and to those who may share some of that same consciousness (for as I said before, my father being human was not alone). I don't imagine that many dramatists or artists care to speak to people like him, to acknowledge his recognitions, which is why you would rarely find him in the theatre. So be it. The work of Schopenhauer, Adorno, Bataille, Beckett, Barker, Kane and so many others radiate toward, rather than away from, that personal experience, not only my own but also that of my father. I am fully cognizant that I am a mere conduit between one generation and another. I am also selfish; I shamelessly use them all to contemplate his life as well as that of my own, fuelling my writing with my father's memory, finding hope in what he may have recognized as utter hopelessness. It is inescapable, for I see him always in the love of my wife's and daughters' eyes.

After Words: Shapes in the Darkness

by
David Ian Rabey

George Hunka's skills and experiences as a dramatist and director are manifested, refracted, in one of the most memorable, haunting and artful performances over which he has presided, this aptly and beautifully titled volume, *Word Made Flesh*. Here we encounter Hunka's notated performance of the evolution of himself, man and artist, through proposition, interrogation, digression, impatience, righteous anger and a sensual delectation in thought and language. His focus is a theatre which does not seek to reproduce or represent life; but to *re-present* life, and the possibilities of the self in the world, in enliveningly surprising ways.

And, having completed my first reading of Hunka's text, I see myself differently, as my own conclusions are challenged, my intuitions encouraged, my refusal of compromise vindicated; in short, this is a purposeful book, which makes me feel ever more purposeful in response. There are moments when I do not feel I have fathomed the full resonances of Hunka's propositions, but I am also reminded that further cogitation and contemplation of his considered statements and dialogue about them (with myself, and my associates) is part of the process: art plays a long game (and is characterized by so doing), not so much "swimming against the tide" as insisting on its own distinctive rhythms of ebb and flow. There are moments when I want to argue with

Hunka (for example, while I work out my remaining years as a teacher, I have to believe that the term "education" is not confined to instrumentalizing instruction, but may extend to a creative bewildering, and further artistic exploration of the unknown—but I probably would not have fashioned that statement if he had not provoked me to do so); and this is also part of the process, because who reads and engages with others in search of mere fawning lionization? (Answer: the despot, whose fixed meanings betray a significant insecurity, as they survey and discredit those who will not justify his or her actions in linear rational terms[1]) (a valued teacher of my own, Stephen Booth, taught me always to answer rhetorical questions, including my own; a helpful lesson for a dramatist.) And I find myself contradicting myself.

Hunka is saliently, specifically purposeful in his anti-despotic defiance of linear rational terms, the deathly logic of mere existence expressed (and bureaucratically and politically organized) through obedient passive consumption. Hunka insists on the right to be creative, in thought and his art; and he demands respect for those artists who *imagine bravely*, beyond all forms and (sometimes appealing) manifestations of "boxes," and who will not settle for less than everything they can imagine, and the time in which to imagine it, and a fertile wilderness in which to do it.

I use "wilderness" in a particular sense. This relates to how Hunka's argument takes its cue from Schopenhauer's and Malta's propositions that our (perhaps intrinsically tragic) sense of the world is based on the sense of the will operating through the body. Jay Griffiths has noted the root presence of the word "wild" in "wilderness," originally suggesting the self-willed, willful or uncontrollable (but subsequently and externally reapplied to carry the reduced and dismissive sense of lost, unruly, disordered or confused); so, Griffiths deduces, "a wilderness is a self-willed land": "what is wild is not tilled"; "Self-willed land does what it likes, untilled, untold, while tilled land is told what to do."[2] In this sense, the theatre which Hunka and his fellow artists imagine is a wilderness, which you approach and project from the scaffolding of practical discipline (but which you do not, cannot, contain or limit: "the creation of an impossible structure," in deed).

In his "Preface to the Reader," Hunka describes his work as "notes" (perhaps evoking both transcribed insights and musicality) "in the spirit of Adorno." What might this mean? It means that Hunka, like Adorno, offers a counterpoint to, and critique of, an ideologically distorted and distorting notion of "reality," which seeks to legitimize its edicts through appeals to progress and enlightenment, but which actually refines and underpins an authoritarian and totalitarian set of terms as to what this "reality" might include, and exclude. This "reality" is cemented explicitly through the allocation of practical (fiscal) resources, and more implicitly through appeal to and invocation of (significantly elastic) abstract values. It may claim to promise the foreseeable security of a given society (in terms of the greatest good for the greatest number—of those who can afford to live within the walls of the state-supported and/or semi-privatized security complex). However, it by-passes appeals to more complex and wider senses of justice and freedom, and shrinks from engagement with terms of *otherness*; and hence, in its insistent myopia, it may be identified as (less obviously but demonstrably) *irrational* in its processes and consequences—even tyrannously so.

Karoline Gritzner's summary of aspects of Adorno's philosophical work is pertinent here: she notes how Adorno perceives a possible resistance to "this ideologically distorted reality, in which culture is constructed as a façade" that conceals an "accumulated, speechless pain" which is significantly excluded from its frames of reference and value; he proposes:

> ... an art that wears the color black. The relation of authentic ("true") artworks to reality is twofold: on the one hand their task is to become equal to the "darkness" of the world; on the other hand they must point beyond this state of affairs, "for only what does not fit into this world is true."[3]

This, I think, brings us close to what Adorno glimpses, and Hunka strives to identify and to find a way to create, in tragic theatre and art.

It is significantly "traditional" (that is, fundamentally unquestioned) that many terms for beginning to think and talk about both theatre and civil life are based on Plato and Aristotle's repressions of irrationality: the terms which have steered us, as Hunka notes, "deeper into industry, administration, puritanism and materialism," towards shinier new catastrophes. Griffiths, again, reminds us that progress is crucially "pictured as a march on the road to the future from the past, as a walking away from somewhere," "for the abstract idea of progress depends, and has always depended, on first, the rejection and then, the destruction of place"[4]—and I remind myself that theatre is a place, as well as a form; a place, or space, that often re-members the destruction of people and places, and so questions terms of "progress." Joe Kelleher has observed how theatre continually "pulls focus" between one space and another: "For example, between the 'given' space of the theatrical stage and the imagined space of the outside world"[5]; and this is part of theatre's distinctively political dynamic as an art form, which includes "its liveness and sociality, the simple fact that it happens *now* and that it gathers people, who may well be strangers to each other, around issues of disagreement but also of common concern"; also "theatre's capacity to pretend, to say and show things that are not so and hence to propose alternative realities to how things are at present."[6] And if those involved in questioning "progress," and its associations of optimistic mobility, are dismissed as ridiculous, unrealistic, reactionary (or "backward"), this might not be sufficient deterrent from asking exactly whose interests destructive ideologies primarily serve (Kelleher notes how, whilst more conventional and anodyne forms of theatre may offer terms of representation that tend to "fix" the relations between things, other forms of theatre seek to "divide and set the social against itself."[7] This latter form might be closer to what Hunka conceives of as the tragic (or, following Barker, "the art of theatre"), which involves dividing and setting *the individual* against herself, and her context. As Gritzner has observed, "to argue for a recovery of the tragic in our age does not necessarily involve an anti-revolutionary acceptance of the status quo"[8]; rather its "suspension of the rational principle" lends a "paradoxical power to negate the irrationality of the world."[9]

Crucially, Hunka identifies how "some dramatists have begun to create a philosophical theatre once again, a theatre that is rooted in the metaphysics of tragedy" (Gritzner: "In tragedy, the claims of the individual subject become general ethical claims in a universe of contradiction and injustice"[10]). Moreover, these contemporary tragedians "link ecstatic sexuality to a knowledge of death," alternative terms on which to glimpse or achieve "a form of freedom." These impulses may to some degree be identified with the spirit of Melancholia (which I have characterized elsewhere as the sensed inevitability of irrevocable loss) which is denied (or else medicinally marginalized) by both commercial and cultural industries (which promise boundless potential gain, though John Gray has pithily expounded on how progress and mass murder conspicuously "run in tandem," through technological advance[11], as well as similarly noting how we have been "reared on religions and philosophies that deny the experience of tragedy"[12]).

Hunka suggests that an image for the proceedings of, and fleeting (even coded) communications between, such tragic artistic initiatives might be that of the monastery: essentially disconnective from the paradigms of the commercial and cultural industries. This image of a secretive, anti-totalitarian, self-willed sanctuary and sacred space may well sustain itself more convincingly than that of a "modern" university (when I gained a permanent contract at a university, a friend congratulated me by writing, in 1985, "These are safe houses, like old monasteries, where not only cant but also a few truths may lurk"; now I am more convinced by the analysis of Alphonso Lingis, that universities "represent themselves as the institutions in which the criteria for common truth is established" when "in fact they submit their projects and curricula to parliaments" which "function as boardrooms where the interests of the most powerful institutions of the disciplinary archipelago are coordinated and transcendentalized as law."[13] Perhaps, on second thoughts, I am spiritually closer to Hunka in his identification, deployment and infusion of the term "education" than I previously thought).

Indeed, this sense of disconnection (from what is prevalent, *dominant*) may, paradoxically, be a means to art, to engaging with others on unforeseen and unforeseeable terms: Hunka suggests that, at least potentially, the "self-defined, self-aware exile has a special access to the sense of the uncanny that produces art"—"uncanny" in the German sense of *das Unheimliche*, the "un-home-ly." A theatre which incorporates this *unheimliche* refusal of familiar terms of recognition and reconciliation thus "investigates and demonstrates the decay of reason and understanding." I particularly admire and enjoy Hunka's conceptual flourishing of "the spectral": "both a fertile investigation of the spectrum of sound (what it hides among its physiological effects) and a yearning to the condition of the ghost, the spirit." This reminds me of the sense I have experienced after the most resonant artistic experiences, that we have a wider spectrum of human possibilities on which we can draw, and which we can manifest, than those which we habitually choose to select and present (in internalized deference to the dominant restrictions of the day): the immanence of the rainbow of desire, to use Augusto Boal's phrase. Also, if "spectral" suggests an ectoplasmic residue, it also conjures forth for me the French sense of the *revenant*, that which comes back, haunting, persistent, suggestive, unbidden (totalitarian regimes are characteristically resistant to the portrayals of ghosts on stage, because they re-present that past's capacity to bring the present to account).

Hunka sets the stakes of theatrical and philosophical enquiry properly high. "To what extent do we allow the language of the state to create our bodies? To create each other? To create our selves? What language do we absorb, do we allow to play or define?" His objective is crucially anti-deterministic (and so avoids the facility of nihilistic pessimism): "The truly revolutionary act is to reappropriate language and the body." Here he is closest to Barker, who has recently claimed "The war fought over the meaning of the body in contemporary theatre is no less desperate than the battles waged in Homer over the hero's corpse"; "Dead or alive, the body drives us mad, and ... only the word can shield our gaze from Utopia's dazzling and obliterating light."[14] I have earlier linked this idea of erotic "madness," a vivifying dislocation from conventional priorities, with what Lingis calls "catastrophic time,"[15] in which ordinary time limits are transcended: what Griffiths alternatively calls "wild time," sometimes manifested in "a resurgence of sexual energy even or especially at the point of death."[16]

This brings us to the role of Eros, its intimacy and intricacy, in Hunka's aphoristic theatre. This seems to me the heart of the book (and of much more), and suggests a possible understanding of the movement from the *phenomenal* to the *noumenal* which might otherwise tend to elude me. Hunka finally discusses the theatre as "the ideal arena for the public expression and investigation of erotic love." Anne Carson, in her book *Eros the Bittersweet*, approaches the concept of erotic possibility, and its circulation, without any sustained consideration of theatrical forms: her (brilliant) investigation is focused on classical philosophy and literature. But I think her ideas may prove pertinent to Hunka's vision of, and for, the theatre. Carson suggests that Eros acts like a verb, it bespeaks the action of an imaginative reaching: when one lover beholds another, his/her vision reconceives them both, in a dual way—in terms of their present *actuality* and their implicit *possibilities*; this "stereoscopic" vision (which holds a "split reference" to more than perspective)

> defines the edge between two images that cannot merge in a single focus because they do not derive from the same level of

> reality—one is actual, one is possible. To know both, keeping the difference visible, is the subterfuge called eros.[17]

In this process of imagining, one "reaches for something else than the facts,"[18] across the space between known and unknown, drawing things together whilst being mindful of their difference; and this space becomes "an erotic space"[19] which permits this reach for the difference between the actual and the possible, "the play of imagination called forth in the space between you and your object of knowledge."[20] As an artful and incarnated place/time/occasion/tension of bodies, saying the unsaid and showing the invisible, theatre might thus indeed be termed an "erotic space," an amplification of one of the most distinctively wild (and willed) initiatives of the human consciousness/soul, which proposes alternative realities to how things are at present, offers "a narrative texture of sustained incongruence, emotional and cognitive"[21] more thoroughly and (manifestly, bodily) intrinsically than other art forms. It is a communally willed metaphor:

> A virtuoso act of the imagination brings the two things together, sees their incongruence, then sees also a new congruence, meanwhile continuing to recognize the previous incongruence through the new congruence. Both the ordinary, literal [descriptive] sense and the novel sense are present ... held in tension ... of an acute and unresolvable kind.[22]

Significantly, Carson also suggests that "Eros is the ground where *logos* takes root between two people"[23] and "something moves in the space between,"[24] between what is and what could be visible—and finds words, form, wings (Brendan Kennelly's poem "The Third Force" offers a further graceful image for this[25]). If Hunka's epigram "Ultimately family is a blindfold for the original sin, as Sophocles, Shakespeare and Beckett had it, of having been born" seems relentlessly unforgiving (not least on the self), his Epilogue gives a glimpse of how even family, like theatre and erotic love, is, with persistence, capable of being remade on our own terms.

This brings me to my other favorite turning in Hunka's labyrinth (in a maze, you become lost; in a labyrinth, you find yourself, surprisingly) in the concept of "dreamwork": "Theatre allows us to enter the structure of our dreams, points out perspective, what lies behind the word, how it changes"; "Spectator and artist become one in the recognition and exploration of the unconscious"; yet "the dream is two-way, paradoxically it reaches a hand outward to touch the world in its conscious expression"; so private feelings can have public consequences, and *vice versa*. I am reminded of David Rudkin's suggestion that the dramatist must be "at the same time asleep and awake, asleep to see, awake to show"; and of Jan Svankmajer's re-cognition of dreams as "those parts of our lives where neither natural nor social laws have any power over us," and are therefore often contemptuously dismissed or rationalized to function within scientifically controlled systems; though they may place us "at the mercy of our own laws" in dramatizing "a repression which we chase ourselves"; hence "it could come in useful if we reversed dreams into reality ... as a certain model for prevention against real repression."[26] This links with Hunka's sense of the "willed nightmare": for what is a nightmare but a drama of how we have lost control over the figments of our imaginations?

If, as Hunka suggests, "Tragedy in America has yet to be invented," this book suggests some starting points, with valuable eloquence. Hunka evidently takes courage from the initiatives of the American artists O'Neill and Rothko, finding indicative shapes in their darknesses. Grateful for their reach and provocations, I will personally further associate his written explorations, in this book, with those of two other properly ambitious American writers: with Anne Bogart's purposeful drive to articulate and extol the power, potential and value of theatrical art and the thoroughness of work (and play) it properly demands; with Alphonso Lingis's energizingly profound fascinations with surfaces and depths, the visceralities of love and horror, the terms of life and death, of affirmation and denial. But I think I will keep it on the shelf where I keep Howard Barker's prose works (*Arguments for a Theatre*; *Death, The One and the Art of Theatre*; *A Style and its Origins*), because I turn to them most often to challenge determinisms and to confirm persistence. We need to know where to find such things, readily.

About David Ian Rabey

David Ian Rabey is Professor of Drama and Theatre Studies at Aberystwyth University, in Wales. His numerous critical works include *Howard Barker: Ecstasy and Death*; *Theatre of Catastrophe* (co-edited with Karoline Gritzner); *English Drama Since 1940*; *David Rudkin: Sacred Disobedience* and *Howard Barker: Politics and Desire*. He is also a dramatist, director and performer, and Artistic Director of Lurking Truth Theatre Company/ Cwmni'r Gwir sy'n Llechu, for which he has written plays which are published in two collections: *Lovefuries* and *The Wye Plays*.

Endnotes

1 On the malignity and ludicrousness of this figure, see Alphonso Lingis, *Dangerous Emotions.* Berkeley, CA: University of California Press, 2000, pp. 43-48.

2 Jay Griffiths, *Wild*. London: Penguin, 2006, pp. 49-50.

3 Karoline Gritzner, "Adorno on Tragedy: Reading Catastrophe in Late Capitalist Culture." *Critical Engagements 1.2* (Autumn/Winter 2007), pp. 25-52(32).

4 Jay Griffiths, *Pip Pip: A Sideways Look at Time*. London: Flamingo, 1999, p. 185.

5 Joe Kelleher, *Theatre and Politics.* Basingstoke: Palgrave, 2009, p. 3.

6 Ibid, p. 10.

7 Ibid, p. 11.

8 Gritzner, op. cit., p. 34.

9 Ibid., p. 33.

10 Ibid., p. 29.

11 John Gray, *Straw Dogs.* London: Granta, 2003, p. 96.

12 Ibid., p. 194.

13 Alphonso Lingis, *The Community of Those Who Have Nothing in Common.* Indianapolis: Indiana University Press, 1994, pp. 143-4.

14 Howard Barker, "The Spoken Body and the Utopian Regard." *Gramma/Γpamma,* "The Text Strikes Back: The Dynamics of Performativity." Volume 17, 2009, pp. 15-16 (16).

15 See Rabey, Howard Barker: *Ecstasy and Death.* Basingstoke: Palgrave, 2009, particularly pp. 15-17.

16 Griffiths, Pip Pip, p. 265.

17 Anne Carson, *Eros the Bittersweet.* Champaign: Dalkey Archive, 1998, p. 69. Thanks to Karoline Gritzner for the gift of this book.

18 Ibid., p. 173.

19 Ibid., p. 171.

20 Ibid., p. 109.

21 Ibid., p.85.

22 Ibid., p. 73.

23 Ibid., p. 145.

24 Ibid., p.67.

25 Brendan Kennelly, *Familiar Strangers: New and Selected Poems* (Bloodaxe, Tarset, 2004), pp. 229-230.

26 Both quotations, from Rudkin and Svankmajer, from D. I. Rabey, David Rudkin: *Sacred Disobedience* (Harwood/Routledge, Amsterdam, 1997), p. 9.

Lightning Source UK Ltd.
Milton Keynes UK

171194UK00001B/147/P

9 788792 633088